GREENHORN

Francesco Pagot

www.theperfectedition.com

First published in United Kingdom
by The Perfect Edition in 2011

A CIP catalogue record for this book is available
from the British library
US Library of Congress registration Number:
PAu 3-481-632
ISBN code: 978-0-9568180-1-0

The Perfect Edition
Communications House 26 York Street
London W1U 6PZ United Kingdom

info@theperfectedition.com
www.theperfectedition.com

To Faye,
because she has never let enthusiasm
fade with experience.

In print by the same author:
BEDDA MATRI (THE BEAUTIFUL MOTHER)

CONTENTS

ACKNOWLEDGMENTS

I would be very ungrateful if I did not thank
the people who helped me to bring
Greenhorn onto paper.

Richard Bedser, writer and film director of
genius and finesse, who suggested that
Greenhorn the screenplay should also be
a novel, it was his encouragement that
convinced me to attempt writing
in this unfamiliar format.

Lisa Cole, my editor, who corrected my slips
back into screenwriting and helped me
to express it from screen format to novel.

Keiko Nagai for being so supportive and helpful
over many animated discussions.

My family, Cristina, Enrico and Elena, for all
the times that I kept writing while they were
having supper and keeping the light on to write
while they were sleeping.

Fall seven times, stand up eight.

(Japanese proverb)

I. THE CAREERS OF LIFE

Predawn that time between first light and night time is too fleeting to be defined. The sun slowly rises as dusty and orange as the desert hills, which surround the silver trailer that is still and gleaming wet from the desert chill. The deep black strip of tarmac underlines the brightness of that morning silver

The trailer is parked next to a highway on what was probably a gas station a long time ago. It is a glinting surreal shape bathed in tarmac, almost a sinking ship against a dark and menacing black sea.

White dust paints frothy waves on the black material. It's dark and dusty inside the trailer. The alarm clock is quiet, a brightly coloured, fat, sleeping Mexican with a large sombrero.

The dials are inside the large hat; to say it is kitsch is a true understatement.

The sound vibrates the clock like an impertinent doorbell. It's a Mexican ballad.

A hand whacks the top of the clock. Silence follows. Pam Horn, a fit young woman, rolls over, grunting. With a husky voice she mutters to herself.

'Madre.., Ya es tarde ... Me tengo que ir -Steph?'

As she rolls, Pam notices that the bed is now empty, but somebody else was sleeping next to her.

There is silence, except for the sound of the trailer's metal expanding under the sun. Pam stretches and slowly gets up. She is fit with a hard chiseled face, blonde but with a dark complexion.

She has a distinctive tattoo on her left shoulder.

It's a sugar skull tattoo which is an 'in loving memory' tattoo, to honour someone dear who has died.

The skull has a rose wrapped around it. It is cute, but in a threatening way.

'Stephanie? I said it's late. I gotta go.'

Pam's words echo inside the space. Pam is about to shout louder when Stephanie enters the room, wearing only panties.

She is holding a makeshift tray with a mug of coffee and bread with jam next to it. She holds it at breast height to cover herself.

She is young and bubbly, a bit on the skinny side.

Her words sound like fresh water running on rocks. 'No ablo Espanol Señor Oficial...'

Pam smiles and says, 'Señora, señor is masculine. You should learn it.' Stephanie shrugs and sits next to Pam. She slides the tray onto Pam's lap. She is much younger than Pam. She has a fading black eye; a fist landed on her young flesh a while ago and left a mark. As Pam attacks her breakfast Stephanie hugs her purring like a cat.

'I love you...' Stephanie whispers.

Pam hugs her back as she moves the tray away; Stephanie's words are warm with affection.

'Te quiero de vuelta.., I love you too but only because you are my sister.' Pam finishes her sentence grabbing Stephanie's little button nose with an affectionate gesture. Stephanie rolls onto the bed.

Pam gets up.

'What are you gonna do about Jake?' Pam asks her sister, grabbing a towel and jumping into the shower.

Stephanie sighs hard. 'I don't know. I still love him.'

Stephanie's words are drowned out by the sound of the water cascading. She abandons herself on the bed, her long legs spreading wide, playing footsie with the sheet.

Groaning like a cat, she falls asleep.

The sound of Pam getting ready wakes her up, and the first thing that catches her attention is the border patrol officer badge shining on Pam's shirt as she pulls the curtains open.

Pam is fully ready in her brand new uniform. Her sister is still lazing on the bed, and it seems like she has no intention of doing anything else for a while. Stephanie can't help being loud as she rolls on the sheets.

'Wow Sheriff...'

Stephanie tips her forehead as if she is wearing a cowboy hat. 'You can ride me anytime!' Pam darts a disapproving look.

'Watchyamouth young lady.' Briskly and a little annoyed, Pam makes a move towards the door leading outside. The warm light rushes inside the room as she steps outside. Dust is already billowing in the morning wind. Pam is just about to go, but stops thoughtfully as if she has forgotten something.

Stephanie appears at the door, holding a gun by the barrel, with an amused expression on her face. Pam blushes, mouth gaping.

'Madre Santissima.'

With a cheeky smile Stephanie is quick to make the most of that embarrassing moment.

'Shouldn't this be a part of you?' Stephanie revels in reminding Pam to take her gun. Pam holsters the Beretta model 96D with a well-practiced move.

'It's a part I would rather forget.' Stephanie ignores Pam's grave tone.

'Go and get them girl.' Stephanie accompanies her words with her index finger sticking out in shooting style and mimicking a gun firing.

Pam doesn't answer and hurriedly picks up her duffle bag. She does not like that kind of banter. Stephanie tries to make up for her flippant remark.

'Sorry... I didn't mean it.'

Pam is stony faced, her sister's immaturity and constant teasing worries her. She would like to hug her but decides to use tough love.

'I gotta dash, gotta beat the traffic.' Pam's words are absorbed by the big nothing. There is nothing here except the vast road for miles, a strip of tarmac in the middle of nowhere. She walks towards a Chevrolet pick up truck parked near an old battered discoloured red Mustang, the only vehicles within miles.

Stephanie leans on the Chevy's bonnet. 'Oh yeah, it's rush hour. I'll go and chat to the neighbours; it will only take me four days to get to them.' She giggles like a teenager teasing and mocking their worried parents.

Pam throws the bag in the pickup and jumps in the cab. Her mind is already on the job, her moves almost automatic.

Stephanie tries one last time to get a reaction. 'Do you want me to... make dinner?'

The revving twelve cylinders of the Chevy churning the tarmac interrupt her sentence. A cloud of dust swallows Stephanie's words.

Dust swallows everything this side of the world.

The pick up is speeding along in the morning light. Inside, Pam is enjoying the drive bathed in the sunrise's shimmering light. She turns the radio on. A comedian with a thick Texan accent is firing off jokes; Pam can only catch the last punch line.

'...because Mexicans will steal the electricity to power their house!' A studio audience laughs. The comedian seems to be enjoying himself. 'Let's talk about attitude. Why is it that a Mexican kid walks around school like he owns the bloody place? Because his dad built it and his mom cleans it.' The studio audience laughs again. He is on a roll now.

'What is a Mexican's favourite Sport? Cross country.' Pam is not amused, but she listens.

'Why do Mexicans re-fry their beans?' The audience is giggling.'

6

'Have you seen a Mexican do anything right the first time?' A roar of laughter follows. Pam smiles at this one. Not a bad one.

'Why can't Mexicans play Uno? Because they always steal the green card.' More scattered laughs accompany his heavily accented lines. 'When you see a couple of Mexicans in a car, who is driving?' The comedian pauses to maximise his punch line. 'A cop.' The audience clearly enjoys it.

Pam has had enough and turns the dial to find something else. There is crackling and white noise then sensible words start to come through the speaker.

The radio is crackling in between somebody speaking in a severe manner. The radio host's inquisitive and matter of fact tone fills the air.

'Professor Arduino has studied the immigration problems for many years. Looking at the recent incident on the border, can you tell us why is it that Mexicans always seem to create problems?'

This has captured Pam's full attention, she tries to turn the volume up, but the result is just more noise. The answer from the Professor is as dusty as the road on which she is traveling.

'The chronic inequitable distribution of income in Mexican society rendered much less opportunity at the hands of the impoverished 60 per cent. Moreover, the country failed to create adequate job opportunities. Adding to their woes was the indifferent attitude of the wealthy politicians, business groups and labour unions. Right from the early twentieth century...' .

The Radio host has heard enough by now and interrupts briskly.

'Professor why are the Mexicans a problem?'

The tone of the question is as sharp as a blade, to the point, but the Professor clearly likes the sound of his own voice and clearly dislikes giving straight, clear answers.

'During the 1940s and 1950s, they forged an understanding according to which Central Bank and Treasury Ministry technocrats were to control macroeconomic policies...'

Suddenly, Pam's cell phone rings playing a Mexican ballad, too loud and clear to be coming from the radio's speaker. It is another Mexican ballad like the one on her alarm clock. Pam is totally absorbed by the radio and is startled by the sudden ring.

She fumbles with her cellular phone, dropping it on the passenger's seat floor. The ballad carries on petulant and insolent.

'Mierda.'

She is struggling to hold onto the steering wheel while reaching for the phone, The Chevy is swerving like a startled horse. Eventually she manages to grab the damn thing but nearly loses control of the vehicle.

'Yes sir.'

Her voice is trembling. She puts the phone onto the dashboard holder and presses the speaker. The voice of Sergeant Hardwood is coarse and full of desert dust. Sandpaper really, filtered by the speaker.

'A third ring is already a bad sign Horn. Never mind six. Did you hear three rings?'

'No rings sir, my cell plays "Los Talleres de la Vida".'

There is a pause, and it is not a comfortable one.

'The tortillas of what?'

'No tortillas sir, the "Talleres de la Vida", it means the "careers of life".'

'I know what talleres means Horn, I am not sure you'll have much of a career if you ride like you are riding now.'

Pam is puzzled. 'Yessir. Sorrysir.'

She looks around the landscape, how does he know how she is driving the Chevy?

Hardwood is relentless. 'That also depends on how you do today.'

9

Pam's answer is almost automatic. 'Yessir.'

Hardwood comes through the speaker muffled.

'Where are you heading?'

'I am 10 minutes away sir.' Pam answers confidently. The revving Chevy almost drowns out the speaker's sound.

'Horn?'

'Yessir?'

'You are 10 minutes past.'

'Sorrysir?'

'You just went past us. Stop and spin around.'

'Sorrysir, I thought the Captain-'

'The Captain is a typewriter legend. We break our hemorrhoids on hard assed cowhide saddles. Our ass cheeks are harder than carbon fuckin' fiber. We are a hard bunch and we do the hard work based on hard decisions. It's not too hard to understand Horn. Spin around and get your ass to the gas station, your coffee is getting cold.'

'Thank you sir you shouldn't have...'

The phone goes dead, Hardwood has hung up.

As the Chevy spins around in a thunderstorm of desert dust the radio programme croaks in the background as the Radio host is grilling his guest without mercy.

'Surely shooting a woman and her child at point blank range is a crime even if they were Mexican? You are not suggesting that because...'

Pam is not listening anymore; the radio is just garbled sound fading in the dust. Her mind is still spinning with Hardwood's words.

2. RATTLESNAKE

The Chevrolet turns roaring into a gas station where five CBP regalia dressed horses are tied to one of the petrol pumps. As Pam passes the horses, she sees one of them licking what seems to be dripping petrol from the pump's pistol. It is a surreal moment until upon second glance she notices the pump supplies water, not petrol.

'I nearly believed it.'

As she shakes her head for thinking the animal was really drinking petrol she enters the coffee shop and comes face to face with Sergeant Michael Hardwood, a tough ass type, no nonsense, leather worn skinned, sitting looking at the desert outside.

He is wearing the CBP uniform but his boots are not standard issue, but snakeskin smooth finish and spotless.

His feet are on the table, in classic sheriff's pose. His men are sitting at a nearby table, keeping a respectful distance, having their breakfasts. They all look hardened and experienced, Pam looks like someone who ordered a glass of milk in a mean dude filled saloon.

There is almost absolute silence in the dust filled room only flies doing what flies do and the odd fizzling off the radios on the officers' belts. Hardwood is chewing pensively on a matchstick. It is truly unnerving.

'It's annoying Horn, isn't it?' Hardwood says this without gazing away from the deserted skyline.

'Yessir.'

'Yes, what?'

'It's annoying.'

'What is annoying?'

'Whatever is annoying you sir.' A long uneasy pause follows Pam's words.

'Suckers annoy me.' He slowly turns towards Pam, it seems to take forever. 'People who suck up to me annoy me. Are you a sucker Horn?

'I guess I was sir. Sorrysir, first day and I am trying to find my bearings.'

'We noticed that.'

Pam realises that from the window there is a good view of the road she was trying to negotiate earlier while grabbing the phone. Hardwood must have clearly seen her while she was answering his call while trying to keep the Chevy on the road.

Hardwood sinks back in his chair, stretching his feet. The outside world seems insignificant to him. Minutes become one hour.

Time has long forgotten that cafe and his occupants. The young Mexican waitress pours more coffee into Hardwood's cup, she must be barely sixteen. Hardwood gives her a long filthy look.

Pam is sitting at the same table as the Sergeant. She is clearly uneasy and fiddling with the leftovers of her breakfast.

'What's the plan for today sir?' There is not a word back from Hardwood who is staring at the desert.

'Do you want me to get the roll call briefing for today from HQ?'

Hardwood gets up with a sudden move, like a snake that missed its prey or just wanted to miss.

Pam jolts back.

'Do you know why snakes survive in the desert Horn? Do you know how they managed survival for thousands of years?'

Pam is quick to regain her composure. 'Because they are cold-blooded animals sir?'

Hardwood spits out the chewed matchstick. 'Economy of movement, that's how. They hunt at night and during the day the stay in the shade usually under rocks, to get away from the extreme heat.'

'With all due respect sir, it wouldn't make a difference unless it was a cold-blooded animal. Dehydration-

Hardwood slams his snake boot on the chair with one kick-ass move. He points to his boot. 'This was a rattlesnake and I know, it nearly killed me because it was a hot day and I was exhausted and dehydrated and it wasn't, because it economised all its efforts so it could strike at any time, day or night.'

Hardwood says the whole thing in one single blurt. He looks around towards the other CBP officers.

'We strike day or night without warning because we economise our movements. We don't ride our horses like you were doing at the Academy Horn; this is not a parade with sobbing mums and proud dads waving friggin' flags. Did your mum wet herself when you paraded past her on your high horse officer Horn?'

There is tension, Hardwood is testing the rookie's attitude and he is clearly enjoying the bullying. Pam seems taken aback but quickly regains her composure.

'No sir, my parents died when I was six. It's just me and my sister now. What you are wearing on your feet is not a rattlesnake but actually a bull snake that many people mistake for the former because it mimics a rattlesnake when threatened and that is its own undoing when it's discovered by humans'.

'You can tell them apart because rattlesnakes usually keep their tail elevated in order to make the most efficient rattle sound, while bull snakes tend to keep their tail in contact with the ground, in order to beat it against something to make a sound. When threatened by anything as large as a human, a bull snake's primary defence is to flee.'

Silence, not even flies doing fly stuff now. Pam is enjoying the moment. The men have mixed emotions about Hardwood and nobody has ever put him back in his place the way Pam did.

Impressive but in an unsettling way.

'Are you a dyke Horn?'

'My sexual preferences have nothing to do with the job sir.'

'Wow. You have a dick then. You'll need all the balls you have to survive out here and the only work your tongue better be doing is licking each others' wounds. We operate as one man and our mission is-'

'...To be the Guardians of our Nation's border. We are America's frontline. We...' Pam was quick filling in, but sometimes silence can be cleverer than clever words.

'We? It will be "we" when I say so. At the moment all I see is "me, me, me". You and your polished brass badge academic first class education are worth jack-shit until your ass has rubbed enough sand up your crack that turds came out like shiny silver tipped bullets out of it.'

Hardwood spits all that out at super speed; then makes a move towards the exit, all the CBP officers move like one man after him.

Pam is still taking it all in and leaves a bill on the table to pay for her breakfast.

The Mexican waitress rushes to the table and picks the green bill up and runs after Pam slightly panicked.

'No gracias señora, there is no need to pay, it's on the house.'

Pam takes the money back and follows the others outside. She is not pleased about taking advantage of her position but it seems a well-oiled practice with this lot. As she leaves the gas station Hardwood is bringing a horse to her.

It is a beautiful animal, all nerves.

'Meet Rainbow. Rumour has it you were first at the Academy on horse shit. Out here there is no fancy riding, only your ass slamming against the saddle all day and sometimes slapping wet at night. Can you handle that? Can you handle your ass being slapped wet Horn?'

Pam mounts the horse in just one very cool move. She is good. She is VERY good.

She stares at Hardwood, unimpressed by the cheap sexual innuendos. Hardwood gets a huge kick out of taking a rise out of her.

'You had better spare your energies and use them on something more productive.'

He says it climbing up his horse using an upside down bucket to ease himself up. Nevertheless he manages in an elegant and consumed way. He must have done that a million times, maybe more.

'You have a young animal under your ass Pam; it needs some firm thighs at work to keep it under control. You need to squeeze hard.' He moves his animal closer to her. 'I am sure that you know how to handle a young male. Don't you Horn?'

He spurs his horse forward and trots into the desert.

3. OFFICE WELCOME

The dust becomes an evil companion in the desert, like a troublesome child who never stays still and manages to irritate the most patient person. It is impossible to get used to it, dust is viciously and continuously changing position, density and coarseness, finding every little surface upon which to rest.

The five CBP officers are riding together already covered in desert dust, Pam is next to Hardwood.

He seems more relaxed now. In the desert he is in his element.

'Welcome to my office 'ma'am''

'I like it, it's home to me sir.'

'You can drop the sir from now on, it slows down communication.'

Pam smiles, it's the first smile to appear on her face since waking up this morning.

'Yessir... I mean.., yes thank you.'

'Don't thank me, when people thank me I look for a concealed weapon. Got a Motorola?'

'Sure, want me to ID us in?'

'No I want you to set it on "vibrate" and play with it.' He seems the only one unaware of his own rough character. Dust never polished that one.

'Do that, I hate Radio Gaga.'

Pam grabs the radio. 'Papa Uniform five, ten-forty- one.'

Hardwood suddenly snatches the radio from Pam, his lips almost grinding the radio's grid. 'Papa Uniform five, ten-three. Ten-eight and standing by.'

The female voice answering on the radio is strangely warm, almost friendly.

'Papa Uniform five, ten-four. Don't get a red neck.'

With a chilling smile Hardwood wears his charm.

'You had better watch your neck with that air-con set on freezing.'

The female voice is giggling while answering.

'Ten-four.'

Hardwood chucks the Motorola back to Pam, he is slightly annoyed. 'You might have only just begun your tour of duty but we have been out since the dew set-tled. Ten-forty-one my ass.'

'Sorry.' Pam is mortified.

The patrol is passing through the small ghost town Costolon next to the border. It is America but the Mexican presence is obviously everywhere. There are very few people around and the ones who spot the patrol make themselves scarce. The few that remain stare hard with menacing and hatred. Pam looks around quite uneasily.

'I do not feel very welcome around here.'

'Get used to it.'

Hardwood rolls up and lights a smoke settling in his saddle. 'You are a greenhorn around here officer Horn and aliens will spot that and-'

'Illegal immigrants.' Pam corrects him.

Hardwood takes no notice. 'Aliens will exploit all the green bits of you and burn you alive if they can. I am responsible for four of you and I have to make sure all of you saddle back home everyday vertically and in one piece. I have no time for lectures in politics and in colour, gender or any other fucking distinction that soft asses conjure up in the comfort of their air conditioned offices half a mile up from the ground where the real shit happens.' He stretches his arms.

'I would love to hold your hand and dance with you in the moonlight and whisper tender nonsense into your delicate eardrum, but I have no fucking time for that. Since we left this morning three officers have been shot at, two are dead; "illegal immigrants" who have disappeared without a trace savagely butchered one rancher and all his family, including children. To me that is the work of aliens, we have nothing to share with beings like that, there is no physiological or DNA shit traits in common with whoever did that. Hear me, Officer Horn?'

'I read you ten Sergeant.'

'You better. Do you want to make it to Sergeant?'

'Sure.'

'Why?'

'I want to protect my country.'

Hardwood gives Pam a strange look challenging her to try again.

Pam perseveres; 'I wanna make Captain actually.'

Hardwood clearly feels better, the girl has ambition. 'Do as I tell you and you will get your fuckin' stars on your shoulders. Just make sure you don't piss on the wrong leg, especially mine. Whatever you have learned during your fifty five days of training you better unload it fast, it's all deadweight that will drag you down.'

'I know Sergeant; I asked specifically to be assigned to you.'

'Yes, so I have been told but I am not going to get emotional about that.' His eyes narrow like blades.

'I am the fuckin' best, not because I look good but because I make everyone look good and I don't mean sexy. I am sure as hell you scored high on all your tests at the Academy.'

He speaks fast, before Pam can squeeze through an answer.

'You did, I checked it out but I am not impressed. You know why?'

'No Sergeant.'

'Because what your service jacket does not say is what you have here.' He grabs his crotch. 'This is what matters. Cojonazos... entiendes?'

Hardwood stops at a fountain, gets off his horse and leads it to the water. Everyone does the same with their horses. The animals' thirsty tongues start lapping up water loudly as a young beautiful Mexican woman appears from behind the tap column with a large basket full of wet garments. Her eyes meet Pam's and she gives her a beautiful smile. As soon as Hardwood sees the two women connecting he waves his hand briskly at Pam's horse, which startles and pushes Pam violently to the ground. The Mexican woman aware of Hardwood's dirty move disappears, fearing the worse.

Pam gets back on her feet.

'I told you it's a young horse.'

'A four-year-old is not that young.'

'Gotta watch it.'

Pam is in a great deal of pain.

'I will.'

'Have you got someone Pamela?' It's the first time Sergeant Hardwood has called her by her first name. She hopes it will be the last.

'Got someone' she confirms.

'Me too, and not just one. There is still a lot to share in here.' He grabs his groin and shakes it hard.

'Maybe you can bring her over one day, she might change her mind after handling a proper tool. Do you strap up a dildo and fuck her from behind?'

Pam is upset; she swallows hard in order not to show it. 'Do we have to talk about this?'

'Relax, ice that tongue. I have nothing against gay people. You see him?'

Hardwood nods to one of his men, a good-looking cowboy type. Pam nods back. 'His name is Tom King; He rides bareback in Brokeback Mountain. He is a good officer and I trust him. But I wouldn't ask him to watch my back.' He laughs at his own silly joke. 'Seriously though, It's nothing personal.'

'I am not gay anyway.'

Hardwood gives her a "whatever" look and makes a half whistle ranchero style. All the men mount their saddles. Pam vaults on hers with usual grace, however the recent fall has left a mark and she groans in pain. Hardwood shakes his head and spurs his horse.

They are on the move again.

'You need to give time to the boys to warm up to you; you are just a boot to them. You gotta show them you will not get in their way when the shit hits the fan.' One of the men is riding just in front; he is a bulging biceps beast. He keeps chewing and spitting tobacco.

'The spit master there is called Buck Cooley. He bench-presses a horse sideways. He is the one you want in front when the shit is raining sideways.'

Hardwood twists around on his horse looking past Pam. 'And talking on his fuckin' cell to his pussy is Dan Matheson, best sharp shooter the Rangers ever had before they pissed him off.' Pam also has turned to look at an athletic built steely-eyed, clean-cut red-neck; the one the cheerleaders go nuts for, talking and giggling on his cell. He waves to the Sergeant with a charming and non-plussed smile.

4. DIRTY LAUNDRY

Hardwood and his unit are surrounded by the desert blankness, moving slowly under the boiling sun. The sky is so hot now that it looks like it is melting and changing colour to match the desert dust. Pam is still thinking about the steely eyed ex-ranger. She stares at the Sergeant.

'Why did they piss him off?'

'Always feel free to ask me anything Horn, that's what I am here for. Just don't ask me what other people's beef is. Ain't no sentimental tour guide either.'

There is only silence, just the sound of hooves kicking dirt.

Pam just cannot resist asking.

'Why did you turn down your promotion to Lieutenant?'

Gotcha, Hardwood is startled.

'Where did you hear that?'

'At the Academy. Everyone knows it.' She lies, unafraid, not trying to hide it.

'I am sure they do.' He pulls on the reins halting the horse and squints into the distance, seeing something.

Pam sees it too, just cannot make out what it is, a distant, horizontal smudge on a bare tree, floating gently in the shimmering heat.

They reach the tree. It is a pale red bra and some matching underpants hanging from the tree. Hardwood gestures to Matheson, who followed by Cooley, gets off his horse and starts looking around. King goes to the tree and takes the garments off, taking them to Hardwood. Pam looks puzzled.

'It wouldn't be my first choice for hanging up my laundry.'

Hardwood sighs. 'A coyote hung the sexy stuff there.' Pam looks even more confused.

'A "coyote" is a smuggler paid shitload of green stuff to drag his human cargo across the border. He raped this young woman and went away bragging about his machismo to his peers. He left his mark, the woman's bra, cut between the cups, on the tree for all to see how big a man he is. These are called "rape trees".'

Hardwood sighs deeply. 'He knows that he will get away with it, as he has done for years raping hundreds. This is part of his business, a bonus.' Matheson comes back holding a T-shirt stained in blood. Hardwood examines it, and then throws it back to Matheson. No words are exchanged; it is clear what went on. They all move past the tree, a silent and somber line of animals and humans.

As they negotiate another dusty ridge an awesome rock spire soars into the perfect blue sky above the pale desert. Pam finds the sight breathtaking as the five riders appear on a ridge. An isolated group of houses appear at the bottom in the middle of nowhere.

On a washing line a few clothes are hanging out to dry. There are some women's undergarments too.

Hardwood stops his horse in front of one of the houses, or what is left of it. He gets off his horse and gestures to the men to keep going. As Pam is about to join the others he raises his hand. 'You gonna work this one with me.'

'Here?'

'Right here, right now.'

Pam hesitates. Nothing is making much sense.

'What do you need officer? Fuckin' landing lights and a windsock?'

'I was...' Pam jumps down off her horse. Hardwood stares at her quizzically and pulls out his gun.

Automatically and quickly Pam does the same, more out of duty than conviction.

'What exactly are we looking for?'

Without answering Hardwood is sprinting towards the house, he kicks the door down and shouts 'Police! Let me see your hands! Down! Down on the fuckin' floor, spread 'em!'

Pam has made it through a side window and find herself pointing her gun at a bunch of children.

Frightened children are staring at the imposing figure of Sergeant Hardwood going about the room like a dog on a hunt. He barks away, froth at his mouth.

'Stay focused Horn, keep your iron sighted, and make sure they are grabbing air.'

Pam finds herself mesmerized by the surreal scene. One child starts crying. The others soon follow.

'Oficiales de policía! Your hands! Muéstrame tus manos!'

The kids are all bawling now. A young woman rushes into the room. Hardwood shoves her onto the floor with a brutal move. Hardwood's Spanish is as brutal as his manners.

'Where is it?'

A young man comes into the room; he has a large knife in his hand, dripping with blood.

Pam jumps through the window and with determination gets the gun to his temple, disarms him of his knife and puts him into an arm lock, all in one cool move. Everyone is terrified. Pam tries to do what cops normally do.

'Do not move... do not struggle.'

Hardwood is almost spirited. 'Where is the stuff?'

The young man's voice is just a little more than a whisper.

'There are no drugs here señor... I was butchering a pig.'

'Don't you fuckin' lie to me or I'll shoot you in the face!' Hardwood shoves the gun in the man's face.

The children are crying even louder.

Pam's intervention seems more like a clumsy translation. 'Do not lie to him...'

Hardwood shakes his head and pushes the gun harder into the man's face. 'He fuckin' understands everything.' He knees him hard in the stomach, the man falls on his face as Pam loses her grip on him. Hardwood drops on the man's back with his knee, pointing the gun to his head. He turns to Pam quickly. 'Check the back room.'

The poor man is gargling on the floor, Hardwood's knee working its way through his vertebras.

'I am sorry, señor. I know nothing...'

'Shut the fuck up. Cállate!'

Pam disappears into the back where the young man came from and quickly returns to the main room.

'The room is clear; he really was butchering a pig as he said.'

Hardwood keeps pushing his Beretta all over the man's head ending under his jaw. He ignores Pam's comment. 'Have you got a fridge?'

Pam tries to help. 'Tienes una nevera?' The man looks puzzled. 'Una nevera?'

Hardwood pushes harder. 'You fuckin' deaf?'

Pam reinforces the threat. 'Don't bust my balls!'

The young man nods his head and points to a corner of the room. Something bulky is covered by a large cloth. Hardwood's eyes narrow, his lips cracking a chilling smile.

'Grab your hijos de puta and fuck off you and your bitch.'

He lifts the man pulling him by his ear and throws him out with a kick in the back. The woman grabs the kids and disappears outside; not before throwing a disgusted look at Pam.

A nervous Pam moves towards the fridge.

Hardwood is already there pulling the cover away. Pam needs some answers more than ever.

'Why did you let him go if you know they keep the drugs in the refrigerator?'

Hardwood is opening the fridge. As he spins around he throws a beer bottle to Pam. She catches it pronto.

'I never mentioned drugs.'

He exits the room leaving Pam holding the bottle as if it was dirty laundry.

5. THE COYOTE

The desert is the usual blanket of dust. Hardwood is laughing amongst the men, sharing beer bottles and sausages. Pam is disgusted by what happened and for being an accessory to it. She wants to make it clear.

She rides closer to Hardwood. 'So to have cojonazos... means scaring the hell out of women and children and stealing their food and drinks.' She accompanies her words with grabbing her crotch.

'They shouldn't be here, that pig was stolen from some farm and the beers from the back of a truck. Those children should be at school.'

Pam nods sarcastically. 'You just managed to secure their future careers.'

'I probably did.'

Their horses find the close distance too uncomfortable, but Hardwood keeps his riding close to Pam's.

'Where did you learn that move? Some new karate shit at the Academy?'

'Jujitsu, we had a new Instructor.'

'Cool stuff. What's his name? Maybe I should go and ask him to try some on me.'

'Her name is Silvia Fernandez; she was Mexico Judo champion for many years and came second at the world championship. She has black belts in several martial arts. I am sure that if you ask her nicely she will give you a good bashing around.'

'Chill out Horn, you did well earlier. I need to see how you handle a pressure environment and you did well. We lost two officers last year, they busted into a shack where they found lots of children and they safed their irons away. Next thing they knew, they were being hacked up with machetes. Turned out the men inside were trafficking children probably for organ donor shit. You must control your feelings and stop seeing them as people. They are all the same.'

'Aliens, right?' There is sarcasm in her voice but Hardwood's tone becomes even softer.

'Look, I know it's hard but believe me you will change.'

'The hell I will.'

Hardwood tosses her half a sausage.

'Things are never what they appear, and what you consider your enemy out here could well be your best bet for survival.'

Pam takes a bite out of the sausage and swallows it hungrily. Almost immediately, she coughs violently and her face reddens as if a Molotov has exploded in her throat. It has. Hardwood is laughing raucously.

'Jalapeños, they are super shit-hot chili peppers, almost top of the scale, those putas squeeze them into everything.'

Pam has the face of someone who is being strangled, her voice is barely audible.

'I can't...'

'Take it like a man.' He stares at the rookie like an evil drill sergeant. 'Ah sorry I forgot no cojones.'

All the men are laughing at Pam's predicament. With tears running copiously down her eyes she decides to control herself. It is hard, though. Hardwood is truly enjoying the moment. His laughter grows like an underground river.

'This ain't a pepper spray drill, this is not the Academy. You can't come and preach to me about immigrants yet not be able to handle a little chili. You are not ready to ride with us, you are nothing Officer Horn, this is a man's game and pussies like you just slow us down. You don't belong here. Go back to your bitch.'

Pam lifts the sausage back to her mouth and slowly takes a big chunk from it. She is now chewing it without blinking, as if she eats the stuff every day for breakfast.

'Sorry Sergeant, I couldn't hear what you were saying. I was having a big orgasm while swallowing this big fucking sausage.'

The men find this hysterically funny and cheer. Hardwood can't help it, the kid has got to his heart and melted it a little. 'OK Horn, you are one of us. You got balls. You are cool.'

The sun is burning in the sky.

Horses and men are negotiating the desert hills; the vegetation is as burnt and orange as the ground. Slowly the posse rides up a hill, going upwards the dust cascades at every step towards them, they reach the top and just below them a surreal scene emerges from the undergrowth

There is a well-gardened little mansion. The green is a real eye-catcher in the deserted khaki background, almost painted in a kaleidoscopic way. A decent sized swimming pool makes the whole scene just plain out of this world.

The men tend to their horses as Hardwood and Pam head to the door. As Pam walks across the immaculate lawn Hardwood whispers.

'Watch your mouth now, no more shit about illegal immigrants and crap like that. This guy lost his wife to the aliens, She was gang raped five years ago while she was in the front lawn sunbathing. He found her in the pool with a brass sprinkler up her panocha.'

'Why do you want me with you?'

'He needs a woman.'

Pam smiles uneasily. Hardwood knocks on the door. Dogs are barking ominously somewhere in the house.

'He loves his pets. You like dogs?'

Before Pam can answer a tall thin man with angel white hair opens the door. Alan Macy, face sculpted by desert wind, seems as if he just stepped straight out of a Sergio Leone movie. He's happy to see the Sergeant, but you wouldn't be able to tell from his unwelcoming expression.

His voice is suave in a threatening way, the tone of someone that has always held a position of power.

'I knew the devil would knock soon or later.'

They move inside, almost cautiously. That was not a welcome. Alan vigorously shakes Hardwood's hand then they give each other a hard, macho slap on the shoulders.

Hardwood breaks the ice. 'Do you still make that evil Irish coffee of yours?'

Alan shows the way. 'I make it only for very few, who are either brave or stupid.' His laugh resonates in a very disturbing way; there is something definitely unsettling about him. Hardwood and Pam follow him into the living room. Everything is minimalist and white: walls, carpets, sofa, and objects.

The whole atmosphere has a cool design feel, but there is no warm touch, everything is empty of any love or passion, like a showroom. Three Dobermans are lying near the sofa. Alan just waves his hand and the dogs disappear down the hall. One is white and before leaving looks back one last time to make sure the newcomers pose no threat.

'I'll go and make that poison for you, what can I get you lady?'

Pam tries to seem at ease. 'I'll have the same.'

Hardwood and Pam sit on the white sofa without losing sight of where the dogs disappear. There are no pictures on the walls; they are smooth like the sides of a giant fridge. There is no air conditioning, yet the place feels cold.

Minutes go by as erratic as rain drops on glass.

Alan appears at the door, tray in hand.

Coffee is served and is the only pitch-black thing in an all white china service. Pam tries to blend in but she sticks out like the swimming pool in the desert.

The two men give each other a condescending look making Pam even more uncomfortable. There is almost a sense of frozen time while coffee is stirred and cups are raised. Everything happens slowly, slower than ice melting, and it has the same cold embrace.

Alan is sitting pouring more coffee for Hardwood who is telling a story that is probably funny but Pam's mind is occupied by scanning the place and the man in front of her. She has her cell phone in her hand and takes a few video recordings of the room without anyone noticing. Suddenly the mood changes, Alan interrupts Hardwood with words made of ice.

'You wouldn't come to see me unless the shit was at least shoulder high.'

'It's cool, it's only shit. I got it well covered.'

'I am here for you, you only have to ask.'

'I will.'

Alan gets up and goes to a desk. He takes out a small white parcel from one of the drawers and hands it over to Hardwood.

Alan's words sound as tough as steel.

'That's a big one.'

Hardwood weighs the package in his hand and seems satisfied. He speaks slowly, almost slurring. 'You know it's a mountain I can't help but climb'

Alan pats him reassuringly on the shoulders and sits down again. He looks at Pam. She is almost frozen.

A "what the fuck?" expression is painted on her pretty face

Alan's words reach Pam like a chant. 'How rude of me…' He gets up again holding the coffee jug and crosses the room to Pam. While all sort of questions are breaking loose in Pam's brain, Alan shifts over to give Pam a refill, but stops mid air. 'You didn't touch your coffee.' He puts the jug back on the table and sits down, right up close to her, real close.

Too close for comfort.

Pam takes a little sip, wincing at the taste of gasoline and liquid tarmac, because that is what it probably tastes like, the DEVIL' S own.

Without warning Alan runs his hand on Pam's fresh looking cheek, ending caressing her blonde hair. Pam recoils.

'Your greenhorn here has Latino blood under her pretty coat, and dying her hair blonde cannot hide it from me. It might fool a lot of people though. Your father was Mexican right?'

Alan repositions himself to better savour the reaction to his analysis. Pam's mouth is drier than the desert outside. She is about to answer when Alan's home phone rings loudly. The dogs in another part of the house start a barking concerto. Alan whistles before answering the phone, all at once the dogs go quiet.

Alan grabs the receiver and speaks into it almost at the same time as grabbing it. 'Better be important.'

He listens annoyed. 'I'll make a call and you will go through in no time.' There is a shorter pause. '…only if I tell you so.' He hangs up.

His attention is back to Pam, like a cat returning to his favourite pastime: the mouse.

'Are you a Christian? Don't tell me, Catholic. Your Patron Saint is Saint Sebastian right?'

His words seem suspended in mid air.

Pam is desperately trying to stay cool. 'It's Saint Clare actually.'

'Ah, that's interesting. She was born in France to modest parents and she was really beautiful. Clare's parents had decided she would marry a wealthy young man but Clare escaped and sought refuge in a Convent where she spent the rest of her life together with other women in total isolation, they were known as the "Poor Virgins".'

41

Pam feels the urge to set the record straight, but her hesitation betrays a mix of feelings.

She swallows hard.

'Italy, she was born in Italy. They were known as the "Poor Ladies".'

All in one single breath.

Hardwood is amused and impressed at the same time. Alan picks Pam's nametag with his thumb and index finger. In doing so his other fingers touch her nipple through her blouse. Pam looks at him thinking what a bastard. He pronounces her surname as if tasting wine, slowly.

'Horn, you came out first with merit at this year's Academy course with Captain O 'Farrell.'

'If you say so... sir.'

'I would not speak of things about which I have no knowledge.'

A phone rings; this time it is Alan's cell phone. He gets up and answers with one quick move, almost as if drawing a revolver. There is life in the old dog yet.

'Of course it's me, it is my cell you idiot.' He is clearly upset; his words come out like a hiss.

'You should not call me, ever.' He hangs up. He sits back next to Pam. Not as close this time, but equally creepy.

'I am old enough to be your dad, so I want to tell you a story. There was this ranger who was on patrol with his dog, a large German shepherd, a beautiful and clever animal. As he was walking in the dust he noticed a pack of three coyotes standing in the shade of a cholla cactus, about two hundred feet away. The coyotes didn't seem to be intimidated by the ranger's or the dog's presence.'

He pauses wetting his lips.

'Knowing that they would scatter eventually with their tails between their legs, he continued to walk towards the pack. However, as he moved closer to the coyotes, they behaved in a way he had never seen before. The largest of the pack started to move towards him very slowly while at the same time, the others began to move off to each side surrounding him. The dog started growling.'

Alan's voice is soothing but cold.

'Now we are talking about a large police dog, well trained and in its prime. Not wanting to take any chances though, the ranger cocked his rifle and aimed at the largest of the coyotes. The pack started to circle in tighter, but still showed no signs of aggression. The ranger was struggling to keep his shepherd next to him and the dog was feeling the ranger's adrenaline rush.'

'Fearing the worst the ranger shot at the biggest coyote but missed, the wild beasts scattered in the desert at top speed.' Alan leans back slightly, his cold eyes transfixed on Pam who feels the urge to say something, anything. Her voice is almost trembling.

'He did the right thing.'

Alan's jaw tenses almost imperceptibly.

'Listen to what comes next lady.' Alan does not like to be interrupted. 'Because the dog was trained to attack if shots were fired he gave chase to the coyotes and disappeared behind them.' He leans towards Pam; his words come out dark as the Irish coffee.

'The dog never came back.'

Alan gets up and pours more coffee for Pam.

Pam can't help but rationalise it. 'Coyotes do that; they provoke domestic dogs so they can chase after them and then they attack them and eat them.'

Alan starts laughing, an evil laugh which sends chills down Pam's back. 'So this is what your experience of the desert is? Just something you read about or seen on TV?'

Pam is trying to keep calm, difficult with someone like Alan who moves and talks like a sneaky coyote.

Hardwood steps in.

'How do you think the story ends?'

He obviously knows the rest only too well, he has heard it before, more than once.

Pam tentatively answers. 'I thought it did.'

Alan is enjoying it, pompously he carries on. 'A few months later the same ranger was patrolling with a colleague and as they were driving in the desert his colleague said that he had just seen the biggest motherfucker coyote that he had ever seen and as they both look through the window this pack of coyotes was staring at them from a hill.'

Alan is caressing a porcelain statue of a dog. It is white and it is a Dobermann.

'Towering the pack was this big German shepherd, all rough looking and ripped, yet still a German shepherd all right.'

Pam is absorbing every word like a child at bedtime.

'The ranger's dog?'

'I'll let you be the judge of that. That's the desert for you. It changes everyone.'

An uneasy silence follows. Hardwood is again the icebreaker.

'I love listening to your bullshit Alan.'

'He is right.' Pam says it without thinking or knowing why. It just comes out.

A sarcastic Alan looks deep into her. 'Am I really?'

'Yeah, but it's not the desert that changes people, people need to change, adapt to the desert, so they can survive.'

Hardwood cracks a laugh. 'Oh madre, she is a desert rat now; from green to khaki camouflage in a day.'

Alan turns toward the Sergeant.

'Just like you were.'

'I wasn't green for very long, broke my cherry earlier.'

'You were once; and one of a kind. Like her.'

'My ass ain't that cute.'

'You were also first at your course at the Academy, not to mention your blood is-'

'That's enough.'

Hardwood suddenly stands up annoyed and wanting to leave. 'Officer Horn let's saddle up. Alan ol' boy it's always a pleasure listening to your ol' crap, just for short bursts.'

Alan also gets up, almost reluctant. 'Ain't such a thing as ol' bullshit... Sergeant.' He turns to Pam, speaking slowly towards her. 'Just bullshit.'

The two men shake hands and pat each other on the back as the old friends they are or seem to be.

Alan puts his hand around Pam's waist, nothing sexual, but uncomfortable nevertheless.

'Stay safe officer Horn, do the exact opposite of what this gunslinger tells you and you'll be OK.'

Hardwood is already walking across the immaculate lawn.

Not a cloud in the sky.

Sun and desert do what they are supposed to do when mixed together: make heat, lots of it.

The patrol is riding along; it is just another day, another rock, another bout of sunburn.

This is their office. Somebody needs to turn the heater off. The posse is heading west. Pam has a silly smile on her face, she senses something is changing.

Hardwood is staring at her, long, very long. Pam can feel the stare, but almost enjoys it.

'Did I do something wrong back there Sergeant?'

'Alan clearly thought not.'

'But did I do something wrong?'

'What else should I know about you that is not on your jacket officer?'

'What do you mean?'

'You fooled me all right; turned up to be mixed.'

'Makes a difference?'

'Of course it does. Blood is blood.'

6. IN LOVING MEMORY

The desert hasn't changed but humans have built on it a convenience store in a Texas suburb. No other businesses surround it. Hardwood's men are chatting up one of the store clerks, a voluptuous looking Mexican girl who loves the attention of the handsome and fearsome looking officers. She giggles loudly and seems very eager to please them. Another female clerk joins and starts flirting too.

Hardwood is coming out of the store with a bottle of whisky wrapped up in a brown paper bag. He climbs back up on his horse after pouring the whisky in his flask. He centres a trashcan that is at least 50 yards away with one precise strike. The bottle smashes inside. Pam looks horrified.

Hardwood speaks slowly, almost drunk, but it seems more an act that real. Or is it?

'Don't give me that look officer Horn, this will make you stand the heat better.'

'How will it do that exactly?'

'Alcohol makes you hotter inside and you'll feel cool.' He accompanies his words with a sip from the flask.

'That's the most fucked up medical statement I have ever heard, sir.'

'You are also a doctor now? That's also missing on your service jacket.' He maneuvers his horse closer to Pam and passes on the flask to her.

'Try it, if it doesn't work I'll be your bitch for a week.'

Another test. Pam reluctantly takes a sip from the flask, as little as possible. With a sudden move Hardwood pinches her nose and tilts the flask in her mouth. She takes a huge gulp unwillingly. She coughs and spits. She is not amused but it's too late. Hardwood stretches back on his horse and lights a smoke.

'That's my boy!'

The Sergeant suddenly regains a proper posture. 'Puta madre! Hullooo Captain...' He is looking past Pam as if he spotted someone important, saluting as if in front of a high rank officer.

'Mierda... What?'

Pam spins around as if touched by a live wire.

'Chill out Horn... see that Bronco?'

Pam focuses on a miniskirt and long legs coming out of the white cab of a Bronco SUV that just pulled up to the store. A gorgeous looking Mexican girl graciously gets off the car while talking on her cell phone; sensual and hot as lava. Pam cannot avoid being taken by the beauty of the woman, the whisky she has drunk also contributing to her relaxed attitude.

Hardwood smirks. 'I knew you like a nice piece of Latino ass. I bet your bitch is like that.'

'I told you, I am not a dyke.' Her words come out slightly slurred.

'Whatever. Have another sip and show me you can handle it.' Hardwood throws the flask back to Pam. Almost automatically she takes another sip, most of it spills onto her blouse.' Don't waste it, a Sergeant's pay is not much more than a greenhorn's, and I can't claim that on the expenses sheet.'

'Sorry.'

The word is even more slurred than before and coupled with a silly giggle. Alcohol is taking over.

'It's still a long way before you can have stars on your titties officer, a looong way to the stars.'

Hardwood whistles to his men.

Officer Cooley pats one of the girls on her buttocks;

she laughs hard and pats him back on his ass. They all laugh. Pam has not missed one iota of it and is not impressed. She tries hard not to slur. 'I have got it under control but your men don't seem to.'

'Don't worry about them, they are the finest the CBP has in their books. They need to get close, to get an ear to the ground.'

'Is ass-close enough?'

Hardwood clearly does not like her tone. She quickly apologizes.

'Sorry.'

'Sun is high and we have ground to cover.' He spurs his horse into gear. Everyone follows. The line of riders is the only thing moving in the heat.

It's a short ride, even though the hot sun makes it feels longer than it really is.

They are in a typical town on the border with Mexico. It's composed of tight alleys and a brick labyrinth always trying to shade from the relentless blazing sun. Pam is riding behind everyone, her head rolling side to side. She is burping and clearly not well.

She leans on one side and suddenly throws up on the side of her horse. The animal is startled by the noise she makes and does a 360 degree spin.

Vomit sprays everywhere.

The men are giggling. Hardwood gestures them to go forward and joins Pam at the back.

Pam is now more embarrassed than sick.

'I'm cool. I am cool.'

'I told you riding here is different from the Academy.' Pam is trying to focus on him. She is clearly disagreeing. Hardwood hands over to her a flask. She pushes it away in disgust. 'Relax; it's water, just water.'

As Pam is drinking she notices something on a balcony on a first floor of a house nearby. She suddenly bursts out.

'Ten-ten! Tenthirtyone! First floor!'

She spurs her horse wildly into a side alley at full speed and jumps onto the balcony. Hardwood rolls his eyes. 'What the f...'

He is staring at the flask as if that was the reason for Pam bolting like that. Hardwood slaps his horse and follows Pam down the same route.

'Horn! What the fuck... Horn!'

All he can see is Pam's pony tailed figure dismounting from her horse while the animal is still moving. She is jumping through windows and up stairs ending up in the building just opposite. Pam bolts through a tented door almost coming face to face with a Big Mexican ape guy.

The beast has large tattoos and huge muscles to go with, he is on top of a beautiful young girl who is absolutely terrified. The man's trousers are already down at ankle level and he is about to start his ugly business. Pam is pointing her gun, circling to have a clear shot.

Her cry is almost hysterical.

'Policia! You are under arrest!'

A little echo, nothing more.

The Mexican brute picks up the girl underneath him with one powerful move and sends her flying into Pam, crashing both of them to the floor in a heap. Pam's gun flies off to a corner of the room.

Hardwood enters the room, stopping dead in his tracks. He decides is going to wait and see; the bastard is enjoying the show. The huge Mexican dives into Pam with a wrestler's splash press to crush her, but she rolls quickly out of the way. The monster lands on the floor as if a bomb just went off. Pam with the agility of a cat jumps on his back and slides an arm around his neck locking it to her other arm in a perfect choke.

The big guy gets up, with Pam hanging onto his back, as if she weighs nothing, he tries to grab Pam with his arms to get her off, Pam is trying to work her choke but the big ape's neck is too big. He finally manages to grab Pam by her blouse and throws her across the room.

Her blouse remains in his hand; he must have propelled her clean off it.

As she lands on her back in an almighty crash she realizes she is now only wearing her bra. She also realizes how huge this guy really is. Shit.

The guy's voice is as scary as his face, his Spanish as filthy as his look 'I am going to open you up with my dick, bitch.'

He lunges towards Pam but she quickly kicks him on the side of his knee, he falls to the floor but manages to grab Pam by an ankle. As he drags her towards him she manages to kick him hard on his face with her free leg. He lets go and, as he tries to get up, Pam undoes her belt and swiftly wraps it around his neck in another choke and drags him to the ground again using all her weight. They both fall onto their side.

'Bitch te gusta a bit of a dance... I am going to fuck your arse con gusto.'

Pam pins her knee against the guy's back and keeps pulling the belt, choking him. The guy tries to get the belt off his neck. Pam manages to tighten the belt harder pinning her other foot to the guy's back and extending both her legs.

The guy's face gets redder and he is making an ugly gargling sound.

The female victim is cowering in a corner horrified, staring at Pam choking the guy. With the other hand Pam gets her handcuffs and locks the guy's left wrist to a pipe next to the wall as he tries to grab her hand. She releases the belt just nanoseconds before the guy passes out. He curls up on the floor holding his throat and coughing wildly.

Hardwood emerges from his corner, applauding Pam in a very theatrical manner. Pam goes to the corner to collect her gun from the floor. She is not happy.

'I hope you enjoyed the show.' She is breathing hard. She fiddles with her belt back on her trousers.

'Not bad, I like your moves.'

He glances at Pam's sweaty breasts barely contained by her sport bra.

'Not bad at all.'

Pam decides to ignore him and turns to the girl. 'Estás bien? Estás herida? Are you hurt?' The girl shakes her head. She crosses and spits in the guy's face as she goes past him. He tries to grab her but the handcuffs pin him to the pipe. The girl stops at a safe distance and stares hard at him. She collects Pam's blouse and hands it over to Pam.

As Pam puts it back on, the girl stares at Pam's sugar skull tattoo.

'In memory of your boyfriend?' The girl's Spanish is pure silk.

Pam cracks a sad smile. 'In memory of my mother.'

The girl gives an equally sad smile and uncovers a very similar tattoo on her right shoulder. 'Me too.' She then heads towards the staircase. Pam makes a move to go after her but Hardwood grabs her arm. 'No statements, we'll be squiggling shit for days on end.'

Pam looks puzzled. 'What about him? We must bring him in.'

Hardwood goes over to the big guy and without warning elbows him hard on his face, and then with a vicious kick he breaks the guy's arm attached to the pipe. The sound of cracking bone is chilling.

The Mexican giant screams in agony. Hardwood unlocks the handcuffs. The brute rolls to the floor screaming in pain.

'You heard my bitch here? She wants to go legal on you. I don't think you want to waste my time with paperwork. Entiendes? Get lost you piece of shit.'

He accompanies his words with an almighty kick on the guy's ass.

The big Mexican gets up in agony dragging his feet.

As he is about to exit Hardwood makes him trip and lands him hard on the floor.

He then squats next to him and goes through the big guy's pockets.

'Not so fast Speedy Gonzales.' Hardwood takes the guy's wallet and money, quite a fat roll of dollars.

He then undoes the gold Rolex from the guy's broken arm. He does this inflicting more pain.

'Better if you take this off; as the arm swells up it can block your circulation and give you gangrene... Entiendes? Gangrena! I'll keep it for you until you make a full recovery.'

Hardwood gets up. 'Shall I leave you two alone? Maybe you want to get affectionate again, give each other a proper goodbye hug.' The big guy is looking at Pam in terror.

He understands every word very clearly.

Hardwood disappears down the stairs whistling. Pam walks past the guy who recoils expecting to be hit again. She ignores him and runs after Hardwood.

'Sergeant! Sergeant Hardwood!'

Hardwood stops and spins around with a 'now what' expression.

'Sergeant... I understand bending the rules and all that but we cannot let him loose. We have to book him in.'

Hardwood mounts his horse.

'Yeah? Under what jurisdiction exactly officer Horn? The local Mexican tacos bar?' Pam is confused.

'Instead of charging like a wild horn into an alley you should check first where you are stepping in. We are now in Mexico and thanks to your acrobatics we cannot do shit here and we shouldn't be here.'

He looks around as if someone might be watching.

'In fact we are not here and never were.' Pam is gob smacked and feeling rather foolish. She gets on her horse. 'Feel good that you saved that girl from becoming a sputum vase for Mexican truckers. Just don't give me more Law enforcement bullshit. If word of this mess gets to the Captain you will have the shortest roll call ever.' He trots away.

Pam follows meekly.

Saint Helena's main streets look like any other main street near the Mexican border, shops are closed and there is not much business. Pam keeps thinking of the wad of dollars plus gold watch that Hardwood took. She is steaming about it.

Hardwood blurts it out. 'What was I supposed to do? Tell me, "Captain".'

'Call the Mexican authorities.'

Hardwood breaks into uncontrollable hysterical laughter.

The men in front turn their heads and laugh nervously. 'You are not serious? Maybe that big guy is the authorities. Actually, tell you what, let me check.'

He pulls out the wallet that he took from the big guy and throws it to Pam. She opens it.

Pam looks in the wallet and there is a Mexican Border Police badge. 'Madre santissima!' She gasps.

'Yeah, get religious. That was one big fuckin' epiphany you just got.'

'That's an even bigger reason to call the authorities.'

'He lost his badge and got beaten up by a bitch, a fija de puta. What else do you want?'

The sun is high, there is little to almost no shadow cast on the hot ground.

They reach a Church. Hardwood jumps off his horse and walks in. Pam follows. It's a small church very baroque and very dusty. A small group of old ladies all dressed in black are praying in a corner. One of them coughs loudly, intentionally as Hardwood passes them.

He realizes that he is still wearing his hat. With a swift move he takes it off, bows and smiles.

The old lady gives him a disapproving look. Pam catches up with him.

'What are we doing here?', she whispers trying to keep up.

Hardwood goes straight to the offers box and thrusts the wad of dollars and the Rolex into it.

He then walks back. His boots are echoing loudly. The old ladies are now all staring hard at him.

Hardwood can't resist, 'I know, I will burn in hell.' As he makes the flippant comment the ladies cross themselves horrified. The warm air welcomes Pam and Hardwood outside the church, a hot embrace as if the devil was waiting outside.

'Am I supposed to be impressed by that?' Pam says it in one breath.

'As if I care.'

'We should have let the Authorities know, we left a young girl's rapist loose!'

'Reporting him to the so called authorities would have got us into a mountain of horse manure for the rest of our careers and given him a promotion.'

Pam cannot believe her ears. 'Is that what concerns you Sergeant, the stink?'

'You are pushing it Horn.'

Hardwood sounds really cold. They both get back on their horses. No fancy climbing this time, they are both very pissed off. Horses are spurred forward.

'You are making your own laws out here, you bend everything more than a horseshoe.'

'Get off my fucking case you green ass dipshit!

I have more than twenty years on the job, my service jacket is steel hard and straight as a bullet and as long as a Remington can reach. Yours is as short and wet as a baby's diapers. While I was filling report after report you were still scribbling Tic-Tac-Toe.'

Hardwood is steaming. He rolls a smoke.

'Here.'

He hands Pam the cigarette.

'I don't smoke.'

'Sure you don't, and you don't muff dive either.' There is more acid than sarcasm in his words.

7. THE CIRCUS MASTER

The patrol arrives at the Mexican border check-point. There is cement, barriers and barbed wire. It is not clear which side the wire is supposed to protect. Hardwood's patrol reaches the border control post near the Interstate. There is a long line of cars going through checks.

Hardwood keeps looking at Pam, not certain if he is more attracted by her breasts going up and down with the horse's trot or by her resolute stare. He tries a softer approach.

'Look, you did good out there earlier, real good. King Kong was a pussy blaster.'

'Thanks Sergeant.'

'That trick with your belt was quick thinking. I am not sure I would put that in my report though.'

'I know; I was improvising.'

'You are a real creative Horn and that is what's needed here, people who can think outside the box, who are not bogged down by the rules.' Hardwood is looking at her like a proud father now. Pam can't help smiling. There is a long lane of vehicles lined up on the boiling tarmac. Hardwood and his men are slowly moving their horses through the line of cars under the torrid sun.

The number of cars and vans waiting to cross the border seems to grow by the minute and so do the children crying, pets barking, people roasting. Nice.

Hardwood looks at the situation with interest. 'This ain't normal; shit's going down.' He approaches an officer holding a clipboard who is checking a red sedan. The officer moves away from the car and respectfully fills in Hardwood on what's boiling.

It goes on for a while; the officer is now showing Hardwood a job sheet and repeatedly points at the building near the barrier where a windsock is lazing on a pole. Hardwood listens carefully and comes back to Pam. She speaks first.

'Looking for someone?'

'Yeah, ten-twenty-nine for a carjacking. Two underage on board.' Pam shakes her head.

'Feds are flying in. They want to see me'

'No shit.'

'No shit.'

'That's kidnapping now.'

'Got kids Pamela?'

'No.'

'It seems that the carjacker is the baby's natural father and this rich bitch from Austin bought the baby in Mexico and smuggled him over. Father found out and went on the look out for the baby and found him. Happens that in the car there was also the son of a Senator's second wife who is a good friend of the rich bitch and she was taking both kids to nursery. Once the guy got the car she fired shots and hit the car. Blood was found at the scene after the car was abandoned.' Pam looks at Hardwood.

'That sucks. Who's blood?'

'Does it matter? Every Government bloodhound is after this fucker's ass.'

'No, it doesn't matter.'

'When they get to him under this heat, they will all have blue balls and wanting to let 'em squirt it for a go, all that testosterone is gonna jack that poor bastard ass big time.'

'You think so? It is probably all over the news; they will not want him dead.'

'Horn, for fuck's sake! News reports on shit like this is like rubbing Tiger Balm on a muay Thai fighter's nuts.'

Hardwood works his horse down the cars column. He senses something. His men are checking the other lines of endless cars.

As Hardwood attentively moves down the end of the column a big black SUV arrives at speed, screeching to a halt. You can hear loud hip-hop music coming from inside, very loud, so loud it vibrates the glass.

The horse doesn't like it.

Hardwood approaches the SUV. It has black out windows and the whole pimp job. Hardwood gets close and taps on the driver's window. The music breaks out louder as the window goes down. A big waft of cool air comes out from the refrigerated car. Inside are two black "homies" and two extremely good-looking girls having a good time.

Hardwood's tone is sharp. 'Pump down the volume son, it ain't a circus here.'

The driver is a display of tattoos and gold. 'I see the horses and the clowns, when are the elephants coming officer?'

Ouch.

This guy definitely failed the attitude test.

Everyone in the SUV giggles. Hardwood's jaw hardens, he starts fiddling with the horse's reins. He is not pleased, not pleased at all.

'Step out of the car smartarse.'

'C'mon officer... Chill out, it's my birthday... Just jerking off.'

'Step out of the car and happyfuckinbirthday asshole.' The front seat passenger leans across his friend.

'Ohi, you can't treat us like that.'

'Again, in case your shit has made you deaf, step out of the car, circus monkey.' The driver doesn't get it; he still thinks the Sergeant is an officer like any other.

'I know my rights you can't talk to me like that.' He waves his hands in rapper style at Hardwood through the window. In one millisecond Hardwood whips his reins around the guy's wrists and spurs his horse, the animal yanks the driver clean off the SUV and nearly stomps on him. The guy is lying down under the horse; he is still attached by his arms to the reins. The girls scream.

'You wanna go to the circus? Let daddy here buy you a ticket.' Working with his knees and boots Hardwood makes the horse rear, the driver is yanked like a crazy pendulum, crying and begging for his life.

'Stop! Stop! OK... Sorry! I am sorry! Pleaaase!'

'Who's funny now?'

'I am... I am!!! I am a fuckin' clown! I said I am sorry officer!'

'I can't hear you, I still got that shit you think is music in my ears!'

The passenger turns the music off. Hardwood lets the reins loosen on the driver. The horse backs away calmly. 'You see? Loud music spooks horses. Didn't ya know that?'

'Ai.'

The driver gets up, all dusty and battered. Hardwood leans towards him from the comfort of his saddle.

'Who's the circus master?'

'You are.'

'Good. Now bow and wave to everyone, show them you enjoyed the show.'

'What?'

The passenger gets it. 'Do it Lazarus, do it man.' Lazarus takes a bow. For Hardwood it is not enough.

'Do it bigger and wave your hand, gimme a big fuckin' clown gesture. And laugh loud.'

Hardwood stares at him hard.

The driver does exactly as he's told. It is quite comical and tragic at the same time. People from other cars cheer thinking it was an act.

A few are clapping hands uncertainly, not quite sure what they have witnessed.

The driver steps back into the SUV. Windows go up. Silence follows. Hardwood moves away followed by an amused Pam who cannot help herself being taken by the Sergeant's bizarre temper. They both end up in the canteen.

Hardwood opens a can of Coke in front of an open fridge. He throws one to Pam. She looks at it and passes it to an officer next to her. She grabs a juice from the fridge instead.

'He was just a kid.'

'That maternal instinct of yours doesn't marry your dyke side.'

'I am not a dyke. I am not married.'

'Yeah sure and you are not on a diet.' He exits the room pointing at the healthy juice Pam is holding.

As Hardwood and Pam are exiting two officers are taking someone inside in handcuffs. The man is much bigger than them, a real giant, and is protesting in a foreign language, not Spanish. He has a shaved head and so much gold on him that he glitters like a Christmas tree.

Hardwood stops. 'What's the beef with him?' The officers halt and respectfully reply.

'Suspected D.U.I. and failing to stop.'

The second officer adds his bit. 'He must be German or Dutch. We'll need an interpreter.'

Hardwood is at it again. 'You are talking to one.'

The two officers look at each other, they cannot believe their luck. 'We do appreciate a hand Sergeant, if it's not too much trouble.'

'No sweat.'

Everyone makes it to the entrance. Pam is curious.

'Do you speak Dutch or German?'

'No and neither does he since he's actually Russian.' Pam is taken by surprise, and then follows them in. The corridor ends in a small room, the sign on the door states 'Interrogation room.'

The giant Russian sits at a metal table in front of a very bored very overweight Border Police Lieutenant. Hardwood is getting comfortable on a seat at one side of the table. Pam is standing in a corner. She does not want to miss this.

The Lieutenant wants this over with quickly and painlessly. 'What is your name and where are you coming from?'

Hardwood speaks to the giant in perfect Russian.

'You know the shit, let's make it quick and you can get out scot-free in no time.'

After a moment of hesitation the Russian speaks calmly. 'My name is Sergei Cherkashin and I want to get Mexican pussy, American women are full of shit.'

Hardwood turns to the Lieutenant and translates. 'His name is Dimitri Popov and he deals with the Mexican Government.'

'He said something about America.'

'Yes, he has diplomatic immunity from Washington.'

The Lieutenant is stunned.

'You are shitting me. Does he have any documents to prove it?'

Harwood switches to Russian again. 'Do you have any Russian papers on you?'

'Like official documents?'

'Anything, even a letter from your sister will do.'

The giant Russian is not quite sure what Hardwood's game is exactly but decides to play along, pulling out of his shirt pocket a paper written in Cyrillic and full of stamps.

'This is a letter from a hospital.'

'That will do.' Hardwood shows the letter quickly to the Lieutenant and then starts examining it.

'He is telling the truth, it's signed by the Russian President himself, Putin.'

The Lieutenant seems less impressed now.

'Putin is no longer President.'

'Must be old then, but shows this guy has friends really high up.' The Lieutenant is not comfortable. He folds the paper and hands it back over to the Russian. 'Merci.'

The Russian seems mildly amused. 'Why is he speaking French to me?'

'Because he is an idiot.' Hardwood and the Russian laugh. The Lieutenant giggles. 'Why is he laughing?'

'He said your pronunciation is perfect.'

The Lieutenant is very pleased with himself. He keeps writing in his report sheet. From a bag under the table he gets a Breathalyzer.

'Immunity or not I have to breathalyze him.'

'Sure.'

As the Lieutenant prepares the Breathalyzer Hardwood stands up and positions himself closer to the Lieutenant.

'Let officer Horn do that Lieutenant, you and me have done enough of those, she needs to rack up some stinky warm breath on her sheet.'

The Lieutenant laughs and nods. Hardwood summons Pam and hands her over the Breathalyzer.

She sets it up pressing a few buttons and inserting a new tube.

As she is about to hold it in front of the Russian's mouth Hardwood knocks the report and pen that the Lieutenant is using on the floor. Papers fly everywhere.

'Sorry Lieutenant.'

'It's OK.'

As the Lieutenant leans under the table to collect his papers Hardwood grabs the Breathalyzer and gives an almighty blow into it. He then gives it back to Pam and whacks the Russian on the chest with the palm of his hand, making him cough.

The Lieutenant re-emerges from his paper hunt just in time to see the giant coughing and the Breathalyzer handed over. 'Excellent.'

He gets the Breathalyzer, presses a few buttons and watches the indicator. 'All clear, he can go, I don't want to have a post cold war headache here longer than necessary. Thank you Sergeant, Officer Horn... Auf Wiedersehen.'

As the Lieutenant leaves the room, the Russian looks at Hardwood with an evil smile.

'He is an ass. And you are a crookedass motherfucker. I like you.' The Russian spoke in English.

'Takes one to know one. Let's do some business, you owe me big time my friend.' They both laugh. Pam is truly disconcerted.

They leave the room and make their way to the parking lot outside. The Russian climbs into his big SUV and hands Hardwood something as they shake hands. He slams the door still laughing and leaves the lot smoking rubber.

Hardwood is waving goodbye and shoves a big wad of bills and a thick gold chain down his own trousers. Pam sees it all reflected in the side mirror of a parked car. Pam has had enough.

It is not funny anymore.

'Not cool, not cool at all. What were you thinking? That guy is probably wanted for murder and God knows what.'

'That guy crosses the border all the time looking for brown pussy. He might turn up to be useful one day.'

'How?'

'What do you expect? Mexicans ratting on Mexicans?'

'I expect us to protect our border and lock people up when they deserve it, Sergeant.'

'You are talking shit, Officer.'

Pam is staring at him.

She tilts her head.

'Don't give me that,' Hardwood says without any emotion.

'Give you what? I don't give you anything, I am a greenhorn. I am just supposed to lick up the side of your lips all the bullshit you dribble. You are... You are...'

She stops, almost broken.

'C'MON! Say it! Fuckin' say it!' Hardwood shouts staring hard at her.

Pam kicks a car door with utter frustration. 'This is not why I joined.' She sinks to the ground, back slammed against the car.

'Why did you join officer Horn? To grow balls? To escape a violent drunk father or a mother who was selling her ass to cops? Or because you never played with dolls and always envied boys biceps? Is that why you joined; to right the wrongs? Well let me break your egg for you, join the traffic cops if you want to direct something up the right way, this is not how it works here.' He joins her on the ground. Change of tactics. His voice gets warmer.

'You are very good Pam, real good, and I don't mean just a pretty face on top of nice tits. You have principles, but you have to adapt, you said it; he who defines himself, confines himself.'

She stares blankly ahead of her. A long uneasy silence ensues. Hardwood gets up.

'You know what? You are right, you are fuckin' right. I am wasting my time with you, you are weak and an arrogant bitch, you think the whole world rattles inside that pretty blonde dyed head of yours. Get out of my sight, and get lost, there is a war on here and I am not sure you know what side you are shitting on.'

8. ESTRELLA

The border checkpoint is still busy with a never-ending queue of all sorts of vehicles wanting to pass the border. Pam is standing in front of the main entrance. The steps are busy with officers going in and out about their business. Two officers are waiting in a patrol car, bored to death and hot under the sun's rays.

She turns to her left. Inside a booth an overweight female CBP officer tapping onto her desktop keyboard while nearby another female officer is sweating and writing down a license plate while arguing with a well dressed well pissed off businessman.

This is Pam's idea of hell.

A horse behind her whinnies. She turns to see the patrol all set to leave.

Her horse is ready. Hardwood smiles, taking it all in.

'If we keep arguing like this we better get married.'

His charm has a perverse connotation, yet he is irresistibly convincing. And he knows it.

They all leave together, Pam rides staring at the checkpoint officers going about their business, bored. The desert seems almost inviting with its bare nature; boredom is a worse fate than riding in the heat amongst giant cactuses and creatures of the dust.

The patrol stops at a McDonald's. The men secure their horses under some trees. Pam is about to dismount but Hardwood stops her.

'I have to make it up to you; I'll treat you to a special meal.' He spurs his horse and quickly they reach a maze of alleys, downtown Saint Helena.

Pam is quite nervous, it's a part of town where they shouldn't be by themselves. Even the horse is nervous, struggling through the narrow streets and slipping on the paved roads. Everything seems designed for an ambush. Whispers and sudden noises make the place even more unsettling.

'Why do I have the feeling that we will be the meal here?'

Hardwood laughs. 'Relax and trust me. I am home here.'

They end up in a little courtyard. An old tavern has the only door on it.

An old woman is sitting in front of the door, she looks like she has spent her entire life on that chair. Hardwood greets her as he would greet his own mama, in perfect Spanish.

'Buen dia Mama Pinta. Como hestas? How are your nephews? Has Ricardo been released from hospital? Do you need anything? '

'Hola Harood! Todo bien, gracias for asking. I need nothing.'

'Everyone always needs something, just doesn't know what. '

He takes few big dollar bills from his trousers, the same ones he took from the Russian, and puts them in the old lady's hand. She grabs his hand with great strength and holds it firm and long.

She is blind.

'You're a bad hombre who does some good, always better than a good hombre who does nothing.'

'If you keep flattering me I'll have to propose to you, bonita!'

As the blind woman is left giggling they enter the tavern. The interior of the tavern is a squalid place with makeshift tables full of the scum of society, bulging biceps and scars worn proudly.

Long knives are part of the dress code here.

Hardwood speaks quietly. 'Don't look at them,' he gestures to the crowd in the tavern.

'How do I not look at them?'

'Just don't. Look at them but don't look at them.'

'Yeah, thanks.' Pam follows him up some steep wooden steps. 'Where are we going?'

'To the VIP lounge.'

The perilous steps take them to a large space just above the main tavern. The room is covered with rugs and carpets, fabrics hanging from everywhere, beautifully furnished Moroccan style.

A breathtakingly beautiful young Mexican woman is readjusting fabrics and clearing some leftovers from a silver tray. She smiles, beaming as soon as she sees Hardwood, screaming like a child.

'Hola guapo!' She drops the tray and literally jumps on him as if it was Brad Pitt who entered the room. He lifts her up as if lifting a feather. With a very smooth move Hardwood takes the golden chain he got from the Russian and ties it around Estrella's neck. She screams again louder with sheer excitement.

'Pam meet Estrella, Estrella meet Pam.'

Estrella squares up to Pam as if she was competition, but she quickly smiles again.

'My casa es su casa.'

'Gracias but I don't want to disturb. '

'No bother at all.'

'You two have a lot to catch up. I'll come back another day. '

'Another day?' Estrella laughs loud 'No way! Relax, I'll make you something to eat. I am sure that Mr Sexy here made you tired.'

Hardwood slaps her on her butt. 'Not as tired as I gonna make you in a moment.'

'No ser un animal!'

She obviously enjoys Hardwood's macho manners though. She takes Pam by her hand and makes her sit on some cushions. With quick and well-practiced gestures she takes Pam's boots off and quickly removes Pam's belt, gun and all. Although Pam is quick to react, she is not quick enough.

Hardwood gestures her to relax. 'It was a long day and it's not over yet. You better make the most of this; we can't stay long anyway.'

Estrella has brought a couple of cast iron braziers burning incense. A tray with some delicious little appetizers and a jar of red wine follow. Estrella's voice is almost enchanting.

'Here, just enjoy.'

She gets really close to Pam, almost to sniff her out, then quickly unbuttons Pam's blouse. She is good, pick-pocketers could learn from those moves.

Hardwood doesn't miss a bit. 'Relax Officer, that's an order.'

Pam seems dazed. Everything seems distorted, loud and very colourful. She tries to stand up but feels drunk or as if she is having a bad acid trip. She finds herself giggling stupidly. She looks at the incense and tries to make it towards the window.

Hardwood and Estrella are laughing out loud. Hardwood starts to undress Estrella.

Pam feels like she is daydreaming, hallucinating really. She sees shapes moving in and out of darkness. Estrella's sensual and perfect body, slowly undressing.

Men, horrible men such as the ones in the tavern are towering over her and laughing, nodding to each other and making obscene gestures. Pam sees their hands touching her everywhere, she retreats and tries to react but to no avail. Everything is like a nightmare of the worst kind.

Suddenly everything blurs white, a very bright white. Hardwood steps in front of her, pulling the curtains and opening the window.

The sun is blazing through. Pam is squinting.

She is exactly where she was laying earlier, food untouched. The braziers are gone. Hardwood is very much in control. 'Good morning Princess.'

Pam's words are slurred. 'Oh madre de dios. What was in those braziers?'

Hardwood looks around puzzled. 'What brassieres?'

'Burning braziers, wasn't that incense that was burning?' She barely manages to stand up.

Hardwood laughs loudly. 'I think the only thing that was smoking here was your brain.'

Estrella is nowhere to be seen. They make it back to their horses. Pam is still struggling to get her brain to accept her reality that seems so surreal. As they approach the McDonald's car park they spot the men. They are waiting for Hardwood, faces quite sombre. Tom King is the officer that Hardwood pointed earlier as gay. 'Sergeant, the Feds are barking all over for you.' King is holding the Motorola.

'What do they expect me to do Tom? Am I s'posed to roll over like an ol' bitch to get my belly scratched?'

All the men laugh. Pam is not too sure what to do; half a smile appears on her lips, more an automatic reflex than anything else.

9. THE BUSINESS

A black helicopter is resting near the checkpoint building, close to the sleepy windsock. Hardwood and Pam are entering the building. He stops half way up the steps. Hardwood hands Pam some pills.

'These should make you sharp again.'

She is not sure but takes them anyway. 'Why do you need me in there?'

'I need a life vest, you will do nicely, and they are all drowning in their own testosterone in there. Just keep your trap shut.' He pauses. 'And open this.' He briskly unbuttons Pam's blouse. She is stunned; it's becoming a habit.

They make their way inside and enter an office along the main corridor, empty and quite bare. Five imposing middle-aged FBI agents are around the only table looking at a map laying on it.

Plastic cups with water are the only drink. These men are crew cut, spit and polished inside out. They all wear dark suits of good Italian cloth, the business, the FBI business.

Special Agent Morrison is the most senior looking. He greets Hardwood first, a cold welcome.

'I wouldn't be talking to you unless they'd pointed a gun to my head.'

Hardwood never misses a chance. 'I'd love to pull that trigger.' He winks. They don't shake hands. There is history between these two; the high tension is clear and crisp.

'Got up on the wrong side again Sergeant?'

'The same side as always.'

Morrison knows he cannot win this one. 'Sergeant Hardwood meet Special Agent Medavoy, special Agent Selby. You are already acquainted with special agent Badlam and special agent Miller.'

'Everyone is special.' Hardwood's comment makes everyone uncomfortable. Special Agent Selby is the greenest and probably youngest and extends his hand to greet Hardwood. The Sergeant ignores it.

'Nice to meet you too, Sergeant.'

'Does your mum know you are out with this bunch?'

Morrison decides it's time to get things going.

'Let it drift. Who's your sidekick? Robin?'

'Special sex officer Pam Horn, first day with us.' Pam shakes hands with everyone ending in front of Morrison. Hardwood has a special comment on Morrison.

'Pam, this is FBI super agent Steve Morrison, he sleeps in that suit.

'Nice to meet you, sir.'

'Same here Officer Horn. I suggest you button that blouse up, we are all aware of Sergeant Hardwood's special procedures but they do not wash with us.'

Pam is really embarrassed and hastily buttons up her blouse. Everyone is staring at her, great. Hardwood has the typical expression of someone who sees things before they happen.

'Are we gonna keep looking at her tits or you gonna tell me what I am supposed to look at?'

Almost everyone laughs. It worked exactly as Hardwood planned it. He is good, really good. Everyone except Miller, he is stony faced.

Morrison tries again. 'Can we get you a drink?' He nods to special agent Selby who quickly fills a plastic cup from the cooler and puts it on the table in front of Hardwood and Pam. The sergeant waves it away dismissively.

'Sorry can't drink that, I am riding.'

Morrison smirks. 'It was meant for officer Horn.' He shakes his head 'You haven't changed.'

'If I had you wouldn't be here asking for my help.'

Miller speaks with pain in his voice. 'Don't make it more painful than it already is Hardwood.'

'It's excruciating for me, I'd rather be shitting crushed glass through my haemorrhoids than being here with you.'

Miller almost smiles at that picture. 'We share the pain Hardwood.'

'I have nothing to share with you. You need me remember?'

It's Morrison's turn. 'You need to chill out Sergeant. I'll get you a beer. I have seen some Corona in the fridge.'

'No. I'm good.' Everyone is nervous. Hardwood scans the room. 'What is the matter Miller? Your suit is too tight?' Chuckles emanate from Morrison and Badlam. Miller is not amused.

'Fuck you, Hardwood.'

A long uneasy beat follows. Badlam feels it's time to fill the gaps. 'Miller is having a rough ride.'

Miller resents this. 'No need to share this, privileged info. This is a need-to-know brief.'

Badlam carries on, ignoring it; he doesn't like his colleague. 'The carjacking last night in Austin happened right under Miller's watch.'

Hardwood is puzzled. Pam is listening carefully. Miller shuffles on his feet then spits it out as it happened. 'We had this broad under surveillance; she was part of a section 36 programme. More than six months of work that sucked more than 600K.'

Hardwood whistles quietly. 'Witness protection?'

'Affirmative, her ex-boyfriend is a big shot Mexican dealer with connections.'

Miller interrupts. 'Washington.'

Morrison carries on. 'Way up.'

Badlam chirps in. 'Wuthering heights.'

Hardwood looks at them with the patience of a teacher.

'Who?'

An uneasy silence follows Hardwod's question.

Miller looks at his colleagues to be sure. 'That's classified. But so high it gives vertigo to Airborne.'

Hardwood shakes his head. 'Go on Miller.'

'She used to baby-sit for this friend of this guy in the Senate, power corrupts the pure and she ends up in the Senator's pants. Before the Senator knows it he is married for the second time to a curvy Mexican babe with a shady past. As things go she has him wrapped around her little finger and to escape the vengeful ex-boyfriend she is red carpeted into witness protection.'

Miller pauses looking at Morrison.

'Not happy because her ex had her sterilized after their first boy she wants her son with her, so she goes to her ex's mama's hut and snatches little baby dealer and takes him back to Austin. Ex-boyfriend finds out and tracks her down, and carjacks two kids for the price of one.' Hardwood shoots another painful jibe; 'right under your nose. So it was you who peppered the car with the infants. Top shooter.'

'We had specific orders.'

'Who from? King Herod?'

Morrison settles in. 'We know this is well fucked up but there are two boys who have been kidnapped by a ruthless drug dealer with a three inch thick rap sheet. It ain't traffic violations we are talking about.'

Hardwood laughs coldly, then he hisses back in rapid sequence.

'You don't give a flying fuck about the kids, you are just worried about staining your expensive suits with this. You just want to pad your high flying asses.'

He makes it to the door.

'This is your mess. You lick it up.'

Morrison's words come out faster than whiplashes. 'We know about Saint Helena Sergeant Hardwood.' It seems that hell has frozen over. Hardwood's face freezes too. The Sergeant stands still; his lips barely move as he speaks.

'I am waiting for the punch line. Better be good.'

Morrison knows his stuff. 'Not here.'

'Then it better be real good Morrison.'

Morrison walks out of the office followed by Hardwood. There is a long uneasy pause. We can hear Hardwood and Morrison talking in muffled tones in the distance. Everyone is staring at Pam.

Everyone is for what seems an eternity.

Badlam can't resist; 'Sergeant's a piece of work.' Miller also finds the opportunity too tempting; his tone is even more sarcastic. 'How did you end up with him? Did you come up last in your course officer Horn?'

'I came first with merit and they let you choose your assignment; I chose the Sergeant's squad.'

Badlam looks around. 'You for real?'

'Very real.'

She feels they are putting her on the spot, and she doesn't like it. Miller adjusts his tie and moves closer to Pam who instinctively steps back. He smiles as only an FBI agent can and puts on his paternalistic tone.

'The guy is a liability; he will slip on his own mess sooner or later and there will be no safety net. He's gonna fall hard.'

Badlam wants to play good cop. 'No need for this. Officer Horn knows what she has signed up for and knows too well the consequences.'

Pam doesn't like it and her intonation reflects her mood. 'What is that supposed to mean, sir?'

Miller's tone is as cold as ice. 'You know damn well what we are talking about.'

'With all due respect sir I don't, and I don't think you do either. I don't see how you can track an animal unless you rub your nose with its shit and you know what it is eating and when it ate what it ate last.'

Badlam moves closer to Pam. 'We know your loyalty lies with Sergeant Hardwood but you should think of your own career.'

Miller warms up; it's a game they know well. He looks at Miller then eyes Pam.

'Forget it, coyotes stick with their own kind.'

Pam is surrounded, but can fight her corner. She steps forward, chin up. 'Clearly your knowledge of coyotes is only Reader's Digest level gained on a trip to the dentist or while watching TV programmes in your underpants sipping beer on Sunday afternoons.'

She stops, looking around before adding a last comment; 'I say this with renewed respect obviously, sir.'

Miller's tone becomes soft and patronizing. 'All we are saying is that you should get out of the kitchen before it gets too hot, ma'am.'

Pam is now in full swing. 'Is this why there aren't too many female FBI agents in the field? All in the kitchen where they belong? I can stand the heat; I was born in the desert.'

Everyone is taken aback by Pam's rapid fire. Morrison comes back followed by Hardwood just in time to catch some of it.

'It seems my agents have found someone who can give them a good roasting.' Hardwood cackles. 'And from what I have seen this morning also a damn good beating if they get too intimate.'

Badlam is not impressed. 'We heard about that. The Mexican authorities are not too happy about it. That ape is a champion wrestler and a Capitano de Policia, highly decorated.'

'Wow, I am impressed. Shame we had no time to ask for an autograph. Fuck, forgot he couldn't sign, cramped his arm.'

Miller turns to Hardwood.

It takes all his FBI years to stay calm.

'You are a sick twist Hardwood. It was a lot of phone calls through diplomatic wires to pacify that.'

'Fuck that. Tell them to sue me.'

Morrison has heard enough. 'Let's get down to business shall we?' Miller grabs the map and some more papers mumbling about something definitely not being present in the FBI procedure handbook.

Outside the tarmac is still hot.

Hardwood and Pam are walking down the steps. Hardwood is in a good mood. As usual he whistles to his men; like a cattle rancher does to his cows. They join them bringing the horses.

From the top of the stairs Hardwood gives them a little speech like a Commander before a big battle.

'Listen up; I'll only want to say this once.

At precisely quarter-past six yesterday afternoon drug addict Rodolfo Gutierrez carjacked the vehicle of a Senator's wife while filling up at a gas station.'

He clears his throat.

'The three-year-old child of the woman was in the back seat of the car together with another three-year-old who is the son of the woman's friend. Shots were fired by the woman trying to stop the carjacking. The SUV was later found abandoned under trees 30 miles southwest. Blood was found inside the vehicle.'

'Approximately 60 minutes later a white sedan was reported stolen from the garage of a residential property three miles from where the SUV was found.'

King mutters hesitantly 'do we know if-'

Hardwood raises his hand. 'Lemme finish Tom. This morning a motel clerk near Piedra Negra was found barely alive after a serious beating. His car was stolen by a couple who checked in the previous night under the name Lopez, driving a white sedan. The woman was later found dead near the Interstate. The ID check came up as Rosalia Lopez, a prostitute known to the local Sheriff. Rodolfo Gutierrez is still on the run at this very moment and aiming to cross the border around here. Any questions?'

Another of Hardwood's men speaks; his name is Cooley, who chatted up the clerk at the liquor store earlier. He is a big Texan with bulging biceps and a jaw to go with them.

'How many Agencies are involved?'

'The F.B.I., D.E.A and the Marshals. There are enough boy-scouts to fuck up quick and good.'

The men chuckle.

'How do you want us to move chief?'

Cooley asks; chewing tobacco non stop.

He spits.

Hardwood's voice changes, even coarser than usual, vitriolic; 'officially with your usual professionalism and clever tactics'.

A short pause ensues.

'My "officially" is hunt him down like a rabid jackal and once you find him don't spank him, scalp him.'

The men cheer. They get on their horses.

'I want the son of a bitch before the sun is gone down.'

10. THE EYE IN THE SKY

Everyone is riding through the hills. A gentle breeze freshens up the tired animals. Pam is the first to break the silence.

'Why did you cross out so much?'

'Not much. They don't need to know the garbage, they will lose focus.'

'Why?'

'You wanna know?'

'I wanna know.'

'The brain works best when there is plenty of oxygen. All the smoke the Feds are farting about clouds their judgement.'

'You don't believe what the Feds told us?'

'All horseshit.'

'Hell, why?'

Hardwood shifts on the saddle, uneasy.

'They tell us all this crap that the guy has connections high up in DC. That stinks of an informant gone rogue, shit and all. It stinks big time. They want him dissolved and scattered in the wind before he has a chance to dish out some ugly jaw work learned at the Agency to the wrong ear.'

'The CIA?'

Hardwood stops his horse. 'You really are green officer. Do you think that they would let someone like this piece of work move through the border as if he were going on holiday with his family? They knew what he was up to and now they have the Senator by the balls. Carjacking my ass.'

He spurs the horse forward. Pam's jaw is wide open. He clearly wants to ride solo. Pam lets her horse fall behind.

She is now riding next to Cooley. The Texan is spitting regularly. Truly revolting and he seems to get a kick out of it.

'How long have you been with the Sergeant?'

'Long.' He spits.

'You from Houston?'

More spit. 'Tomball.'

'Close enough.' Another spit misses her face by less than an inch.

'Welcome aboard and all that. Can you bounce your tits near someone else now?' He spits.

'Sorry for busting your chops officer Cooley. Jeez.' She spits as well then spurs her horse forward and flanks King, the good looking gay guy. He is very friendly, and doesn't spit. 'Never mind Cooley, he'll warm up to you. He needs the woman inside him to wake up and tell him what he is.'

Pam smiles. 'He'll bite your head off if he hears you saying that.'

'He might bite off more than what his big jaws can chew.' They both laugh like naughty teenagers. The desert is changing, more bushes and a bit more green starts to show, not much but enough to give hope.

A ranch appears in the distance, some trees and some fields with crops. Nothing weird or peculiar and is maybe that why it all seems rather staged.

A fountain sits in the middle of the courtyard.

Agricultural tools and tractors are scattered around, but like a display, not as if someone is really using them. The men get their horses to the water pump, Hardwood gestures Pam to follow him to the barn.

As they enter it's very clear why this is not a typical farm. The barn is crammed with monitors and high tech equipment.

A drone sits in the middle, surrounded by technicians busy downloading data and doing final pre-flight checks. It is very high tech and totally unexpected. The Sergeant moves with familiar ease, he has clearly been there before, more than once. 'I bet you did not spot this in the tourist guide book.'

Pam is genuinely in awe. 'Impressive, to say the least.'

'Fuckin' useless at the most. Isn't that the absolute truth Carradine?'

A bespectacled man in a white coat, hale but somewhat bookish is walking towards them with an electronic note pad. 'Absolute truth is fool's belief. One day you might understand how absolutely obsolete you are Hardwood.'

'One day that flying fridge might complete a mission alright.'

Carradine smiles at Pam. 'Nice to meet you Officer?...' pam smiles back; 'Horn, but call me Pam. That is the Silver Arrow Hermes 450 right?'

Carradine beams with happiness. 'How refreshing to have someone who doesn't swear or spit every second or behave like a horny stallion and has a brain that actually processes information, not just orders the heart to beat. Don't tell me that you are part of his posse.'

Pam looks amused. She is about to answer when Hardwood does the usual Sergeant's thing.

'We're fuckin' wasting time, what shit have you got for me?'

Carradine shakes his head in disbelief, pointing all fingers towards Hardwood. 'As if to prove my point; anyway, the 'flying fridge' picked up some activity last night that you might want to see.' They move next to a monitor. Carradine presses a few buttons. A night-vision high resolution image fills the screen. A ghostly white figure seems to be negotiating the undergrowth.

'What is this some kind of joke? Some perv looking for some action, that's all.'

Carradine sighs. 'Hold your horse cowboy.'

He presses a few more buttons. The image is magnified and slowed down. At one point we can clearly see two dots coming out of the man's body. Two small heads. Kids' heads.

This definitely gets Hardwood's full attention. 'Holy shit. Who else has seen this?'

'Just the three of us. But I can't withhold it for long.'

Hardwood leans forward. 'What's the coordinates? '

Carradine bites his lips. 'That's the embarrassing moment.' He moves to the side and starts tapping nervously on his notepad.

'The weak radar backscatter from surrounding vegetation interfered with the twin tail-booms, while the 90-MHz antenna pod-mounted on wingtip was out of service. All Gyro-star metadata are corrupted.'

Hardwood looks at him puzzled; the gyro what? 'You know fuck all.'

Carradine takes the comment on the chin sighing deeply. 'As Hardwood here would say.'

'Show me the lead up to that.'

Carradine presses even more buttons. The image rewinds and suddenly a familiar site appears on the monitor; a mansion, a swimming pool. Three dogs strolling on a well kept lawn. Pam stares at the screen, she knows exactly what and where that is. Carradine is observing the Sergeant instead of the screen.

'You know where it is Hardwood? '

The answer comes briskly. 'No idea; could be anywhere. Sort out the data and radio us in when you have that location.'

Pam is startled. 'But Sergeant the...'

Hardwood darts a look that cannot be misinterpreted. Shut the fuck up. He then smiles at Carradine.

'Radio us professor. We are moving.' He presses Pam on her shoulders, time to leave. They cross the courtyard exiting the barn.

Hardwood is walking fast, almost running. Pam is struggling to keep up.

'Officer Horn you need to get your shit squared. Don't make me regret accepting you into my unit. That can change very quickly.'

They reach the space where his men have stationed the horses. Hardwood barks away. 'If we are gonna bust that sonofabitch ass today, we need to get suited up properly and have some extra toys with us.'

Cooley can't help being Cooley. 'Yeahhhh. Rodeo time.'

They all move to one of the buildings opposite the barn. Outside it looks like any other building facing the courtyard, wooden and charming, but as they walk through the main door there is a meter thick concrete wall, containing row after row of all sorts of weapons and tactical vests, body armour and the whole SWAT paraphernalia that make boys happy. A burly sergeant called O'Hara greets Hardwood.

'Hardwood, what the fuck's going on? Forgot to pay the last check?'

'O'Hara old fart. All cool and dandy. I need to suit up my ladies here.'

'If you think you can get away with it and you scribble that ugly cross you call your signature, sure!'

O'Hara is now looking at Pam 'Who's this?'

'Pam Horn, nice to meet you.'

'Sergeant O'Hara, but friends call me Tank. Nice to meet you ma'am, you don't belong to that motley crew, you got class.'

Hardwood is in a hurry.

'You gonna ask her out so we can get moving or what?'

O'Hara gets the message and everyone gets to their business super quick. It's a drill they know well. O'Hara tries to make some small talk but everyone keeps themselves to themselves.

'It looks like you are gonna give someone some serious lead. Are you starting a war or something?'

Sergeant O'Hara awaits an answer but nobody pays him any attention, they are way to busy playing with the new toys and getting ready. In a single line they all leave. Hardwood leaves a dollar bill on the desk.

'Keep the change boy.'

'You are a funny man Hardwood, make sure you get a bigger audience than coyotes, you deserve better.'

O'Hara chuckles to himself and gets back to his daily task, filling in paperwork.

Laden with the extra tactical gear, Hardwood and his crew are riding in a line silhouetted against the bright sun.

They look fearsome like the Horsemen of the Apocalypse. Pam is riding next to Matheson. She cannot get out of her mind what was said by the FBI suits in that room.

'What happened in Saint Helena with the Sergeant?' Matheson's answer is as rough as his neck.

'You are asking the wrong guy, I am spraying no shit on anybody.'

He spurs his horse forward.

11. LESSON LEARNED

A black Doberman makes no noise, except for a subtle panting as it walks down the hall. It is one of Alan's beasts. The elegant animal turns into its master's mansion sitting room. The dog goes straight to an armchair and stops. Its tongue is licking something, a man's hand dripping blood. A growl is heard from behind and the dog retreats fast away from the hand.

Alan is sitting in his white lounge, caressing his white Doberman. The dog stops growling and seems relaxed and so does Alan. A thirty something gang tattooed Mexican is sitting opposite. His white shirt is stained in blood, his jeans ripped in few places. The guy looks like a right royal mess. Oddly though, he seems relaxed.

As he tries to adjust himself on his armchair the Doberman lifts his head and starts growling.

The growl increases with the man attempting to shift further onto his side to ease the pain. His hand is red with blood. Alan speaks with unnatural calm.

'Dobermans are very clean and they cannot stand stains. Rodolfo... right?'

The guy nods. Yes.

'I thought so. You have to relax as much as you can otherwise Blanko gets nervous and he plays games.' Alan leans back.

'You brownies love pit bulls, rottweilers, big fuckin' stupid dogs. Dobermans are different, they are genetically engineered; they are designed; designed to be smart. They figure things out and they always get what they want.'

'They are very clean dogs Dobermans, they toilet themselves as a cat does, they hate mud and dirt. They are the felines of the dog world. They move like a panther, they roar like a tiger, they are as fast as a leopard and as powerful as a lion.'

Alan gets up and Blanko gets up on all fours at the very same precise time, not one second late, in perfect synchronism. Alan starts walking around the sofa and the armchair where Rodolfo Gutierrez is sitting, the Doberman shadows every step.

Alan continues his lecture.

'They are copycats; they mimic everything their owner does. They become one with their master. They think like their owners.' Alan stops right in front of Rodolfo. 'They think and they learn.'

Rodolfo doesn't know what to answer. Blanko is growling. Alan starts pacing around again, but Blanko stays right in front of the Mexican. Alan goes to a drawer on his desk, pulls out a gun. He chucks the gun on Rodolfo's lap, who winces; it's a heavy gun. He slowly grabs it. Blanko is growling louder.

'You make a mess and you come here asking for help. How long have you been working for me?' Rodolfo's answer is barely audible. He just mutters something.

'Can't hear you.'

'Four... years.'

'Blanko has learned from me in two years more than you did in double that time. Where does that leave you.. dog?'

'Sorry.'

'You fuckin' better be.'

Alan swears for the first time during their conversation. He is really pissed off. Alan gestures Rodolfo to leave. The Mexican is way too happy to oblige. Blanko doesn't miss a single move.

Alan's cellular phone rings. 'Yes.' He listens carefully. 'I am only the man in the middle, I hear nothing.'

He hangs up and slowly moves close to the large French windows overlooking his immaculate lawn. Outside the automatic sprinklers pops out from the ground and water the perfectly green lawn.

'Water, Blanko, we need some water.' He caresses the faithful animal on the head without looking at it, and then he disappears into the adjacent room.

The artificial rains brings an unnatural calm.

Through the water jets of the sprinkling systems Hardwood's unit is moving through the freshly wet lawn. Hardwood reaches the front door accompanied by Pam; she is alert and gives him cover. They are all wearing their full tactics forced entry kits, Robocop style. He rings the doorbell. We can hear the bell inside going off; again, longer. No other sounds.

Pam whispers. 'There's no barking.'

Hardwood cocks his shotgun, gesturing a nervous looking Pam to step aside.

He nods to Matheson and Cooley to go to the back; he waves King to give them cover. Everyone moves like the well-trained officers they are. Suddenly the door opens, Alan appears on the doorframe, wearing a bathrobe and dripping water.

'Come in, I was expecting you. Not quite so early though. Come on in.' Hardwood makes the shotgun safe. Pam relaxes; almost. 'We didn't hear the dogs.'

'They heard you alright.' Blanko appears from behind his owner, a faithful shadow.

'They are trained not to bark after dusk. With all the scavengers surfacing at night they would give me a permanent concert.' Alan is looking at the kit that they are wearing.

'Who are you expecting? Godzilla?' He disappears inside without waiting for an answer.

Hardwood looks around and then walks behind Alan, followed by Pam who is followed by Blanko.

The white sitting room is paler than ever.

'Make yourself at home.' Alan indicates at the sofa.

'Do you mind?' he gestures at the tactical kit they are wearing, full of desert dust and dirty.

Hardwood drops his kit on the floor and sits on the armchair were Rodolfo was sitting earlier. Pam reluctantly follows his actions while looking at her Sergeant expecting him to say something but instead he waves his hand at her as if to say 'you explain'. She is not sure but decides to give it a go.

'Sir... we received intelligence that... there is the possibility that a-'

'He was here wasn't he?' Hardwood's words cut Pam short. She freezes. Alan sits in the armchair adjusting his bathrobe. Stony faced.

Hardwood doesn't give up easily. 'How long can guys like you jerk everyone off without getting horse-fucked themselves?'

Pam is totally lost for words. Hardwood clearly is not. 'Are you packin'?'

Alan stands up slowly, opens the bathrobe and lets it fall on the floor. He is stark naked. Pam is not enjoying the show.

'Sergeant, what the f....?'

Alan speaks calmly. 'No I am not and yes, he was here.' He sits down again, just as Mother Nature made him, impervious.

'This is bigger than you and me Mike. Don't even get between that because it's too big. We can make it all go away. We can take care of it. We can take good care of you; both of you.'

Pam is stunned.

'Sergeant? Sergeant what the fuck is...?'

Hardwood stares hard.

'That's what you do Alan, don't you? Make it go away. You are a pain killer. Is that what you tell them? Do you tell them that it's not going to hurt?'

Pam gets up; she has never been so uncomfortable in her life. 'I am not sure what I am listening to here, but I am damn sure I am not comfortable with this, someone better start talking fuckin' sense.'

Alan is irritated but his voice is still soft. 'Sit down, please. I understand how this can make you uncomfortable but there is no reason to be rude. Sit down… please.' An uneasy silence follows.

Pam's brain is racing.

'Fuck you…. Fuck you all.'

She makes a move towards the door but one of Alan's Dobermans appears right in front of her, growling. With incredible speed she whips out her Beretta from the holster and aims it at the growling dog.

'Sir, just call back your dog or I'll have to shoot it. Sir…' The second Doberman materializes behind her, growling even louder, half an inch away from her genitals. Alan's voice is even calmer, words almost spelled out. 'You can shoot Hermes but Athena will tear you apart at the first gunshot. Just sit back and relax, it will all make sense in a minute.'

'Sir, I am going to ask you one more time. Call back your dog.' Her hand is trembling but the Beretta is aimed straight at the dog's forehead. Out of nowhere Blanco jumps at Pam's hand and grabs her gun.

The movement is lightening fast as his sharp teeth graze Pam's hand. Alan smiles imperceptibly.

'Dobermans are great thieves officer. Would you mind sitting down now?'

Pam looks at Hardwood who nods conceding. Holding her bleeding hand Pam sits down slowly like a child who's been told off. Blanco trots to Pam with her gun in his mouth. Very gently the white Doberman drops the gun at Pam's feet, then disappears into the hall.

Drops of Pam's blood start falling on the pure white carpet. Alan is irritated by it. Pam slouches back in the armchair.

'Watch the carpet please.'

Pam rests her hand on the armchair but drags it first along the precious white furnishing fabric, smearing it slowly, purposely trying to unnerve him.

Alan looks at the red spread in horror. He hisses words, truly pissed off. 'Women... They always bleed to make us feel bad about everything; to remind us once a month that they suffer to give birth. They use blood as an excuse to faint or as a powerful grip on their offsprings; -they are my blood-. Their monthly visitor is used as an excuse for not going to school or work, or avoiding the gym or even better, avoiding sex. Blood is the perfect manipulating tool women have, the ultimate control dial. Do you suffer from hyper-menorrhagia officer Horn or you just cannot handle the extra flow of estrogens in your blood?'

Pam's wit is as always as fast as her gun dexterity. 'I can handle it. Can you handle women sir? Grown up, fully formed, self asserting women?'

Hardwood chuckles. 'She fucked you up good Alan, kid got balls.' Pam looks at Hardwood as if to say 'What side are you on?'

'You're fuckin' wasting my time Alan. What are you offering? Or shall I talk to someone who is really in charge? I am sick of dealing with peons. I need to get to whoever's in charge.' Hardwood's voice trembles with rage.

'Nobody knows. Nobody gets the big picture.'

'No, you don't get it, you are nothing, just a pathetic twisted faggot sonofabitch who likes to play queer games because you cannot get it up no more. Go fuck yourself.' He stands up. The two Dobermans growl.

'You are breaking my heart Mike. You have no idea how fragile I am right now. But I still want to help you. I can take care of your career, even your life; give you a nice fat bank account in the Caymans. I can take care of Saint Helena and I can take care of wonderwoman here as well.'

Hardwood has heard enough. 'You are not taking care of anyone. My greenhorn here has bigger balls than you'll ever have. Everything you took care of ended up rotting, including your poor Patricia. You have got a magic touch that transforms gold into shit.' He inches forwards. Dogs growl louder.

'Now me and my officer are gonna walk out of that door and your pooches better behave otherwise you should consider redecorating here.'

The dogs growl even louder. Then suddenly all hell breaks loose, shotgun blasts and gunpowder fill the room. The dogs fly onto the furniture like blasted rag dolls, blood sprays everywhere. Matheson and Cooley make their appearance, shotguns smoking, the cavalry has arrived.

Cooley smirks. 'Hate fuckin' vermin.'

He spits on the white floor right next to Alan's foot. A big blotch of disgusting slimy black tobacco lands with devastating effect. Alan stays where he is; a tear runs down his left cheek.

Hardwood wants to have the last word. 'Don't go French on me now Alan, I did ask you, with sugar on top.'

No answer. Alan stares ahead, still sitting, still naked. 'Make yourself decent, I'll be seeing you.'

The Sergeant looks at the walls covered by Doberman remains. 'Sorry about the mess.' Hardwood picks up his tactical kit and walks out followed by Pam after she picks up her weapon from where Blanco dropped it. Cooley spits again on the carpet, Matheson giggles and they exit too.

The grass is still wet.

They walk tall on Alan's mansion lawn. The sunset bathes them in heroic light. Gorgeous sunrays shimmering make everything look golden and precious. The group is walking back in silence to their horses. Cooley and Matheson are messing about mimicking the dogs being blasted away. King is joining in coming from another side. Pam is walking next to Hardwood.

'Welcome on board officer Horn, you passed the big boys 'test'.'

'I'll pass on that Sir.'

'What do you mean?' They stop near the pool.

'You heard me before, I didn't sign up for this.'

Hardwood stares at her as if he's about to hit her. He looks at his wristwatch, wants to make a point.

'Fuckin' hey. You just tucked twelve under your belt. Congratulations.' He stares at Pam, a hard gaze.

'Shame it's 'twelve' hours compared to my twenty-four freaking' years of this shit. You are a piece of work Horn. You're something.'

He shakes his head in disgust.

'It takes all kinds, sir.'

'And what kind that would be? Huh?'

'You tell me, because what I have seen so far is seriously fucked up.'

All the men are now around Pam. Matheson, Cooley and King. They look nervous, they clearly don't like what they hear. Hardwood looks around and smiles.

'You are making the boys nervous.'

'Tough, it's good for their blood circulation. More oxygen to the brain; clears the thinking process.'

'What makes you judge and jury all of a sudden?'

'What makes you above the law?'

'The Law? The Lawwwwww?'

Everyone giggles nervously, only Pam is serious.

'I tell you officer Horn what your fuckin' law means to people like Mr White in there. It means jackshit. He wipes his ass with your regulations and protocols. He is the law. He was with the Agency for so many years that they named a department after him. He has most people on Capital Hill sucking up to him to take care of shit.'

'Your shit too.' Hardwood pauses knowing too well she refers to the package he gave him last time.

'That's a private matter.'

'Yeah sorry, I forgot, I am only a woman and a greenhorn. Sure, what would I know about corruption and bent officers? I am too green.'

Cooley sides with the Sergeant and wants to make it clear. 'Watch you mouth lady.' He spits and catches Pam on her cheek with his black sputum.

WHACK! Pam nails the Texan's massive jaw. Cooley staggers almost falls. Cooley drops his shotgun and moves towards her frothing at the mouth. 'I'll kill ya!'

He swings an overhead punch that Pam catches mid flight and with amazing grace she turns into an arm lock and then a perfect throw, sending Cooley flying. The Texan falls with an almighty splash in the pool. He emerges fuming with rage, extracts his gun and points it at Pam. 'You fuckin' bitch!'

Hardwood steps into the line of fire, shielding Pam. 'Start swimming Tarzan and put that iron away before you embarrass yourself even more.'

Cooley swats the surface with his gun and swims to the edge of the pool; slowly climbs out, drenched. Matheson and King exchange looks. They don't know if it's funny or not. There is a lot of tension.

They all go to their horses.

Hardwood is amused. 'I don't think any of them will ask you out after this.'

They also move towards their horses. Pam sighs.

'I am out. No more of this, it can't be like this.'

Hardwood starts laughing loud, hysterically loud, uncontrollable. His men look back, they never seen him like that. They join giggling nervously.

'You are a fucking riot Horn.'

He wipes laughter tears off his eyes. 'I have got some bad news and some more bad news for you. It is like this. What were you expecting? Riding into town and the bad guys shitting themselves as your shadow casts over them? Women and children looking at you with puppy eyed devotion and eternal admiration?'

He stops.

His words are sinking hard into officer Horn. He is right and he knows that she knows it.

Hardwood almost spells it out.

'This is the border officer Horn, wars start at the border, not in the middle of towns.'

She snaps.

'What war Sergeant? Your "personal" war? What's your personal beef with immigrants? Maybe because you mother was from Russia?'

Hardwood stares hard at Pam. 'My parents were Polish, but my mother was a Russian teacher and spoke Russian at home. Satisfied?'

He is standing next to his horse, patting the animal's head nervously. This is very uncomfortable for Sergeant Hardwood. He has a burden he needs to unload.

'My mother wanted my father to become Russian; she wanted all of us to become Russian. She was convinced Russia was going to invade Poland and if we spoke perfectly we'd be spared. She eventually left us for a Russian naval Officer. I was three years old. My father left for the USA and made sure there was no trace of what we were anymore, even changing his surname after marrying a woman from Texas. He killed himself shortly after.'

A long uneasy silence ensues, Pam sees a side of Hardwood she hasn't seen before.

'My dad was from Arizona, not Mexico, my mum was. She died when I was born. My dad remarried an ol' hometown sweetheart and had another girl with her. My step mum tried to wipe out all traces of Mexican in me but the more she'd try the more Mexican I felt.'

'No shit? You're all fucked up.'

'Thanks.'

'No sweat.' Hardwood is back to his usual self. He gives out a chilling smile.

The sun is almost setting.

The light is so beautiful that it could make anyone fall in love. 'What is it gonna be officer Horn? Are you gonna give me shit? First day on the job and you are already quitting?'

They all get on their horses. Pam is silent. They are on the move.

12. CHILD' S PLAY

Saint Helena's downtown is soaked by the descending evening, the air is still warm but not for long. Hardwood's unit is passing through. Amidst the alleys, women talk to women basking in the evening mounting breeze. Two children are playing with a ragged ball.

The sounds of television sets broadcasting in Spanish filter through open windows filling the air, overlapping in a cacophony of surreal compositions.

A football match is taking a sudden disappointing twist and a small crowd gasps disappointed.

A soap opera is in the midst of a cliff-hanger set up. A surreal calm bathes the narrow streets.

Hardwood's posse is coming through observing from the height of their mounts, tired and dusty, ghost riders surviving another day. Pam is riding last, deep in thought.

She looks around with mixed emotions, almost trying to absorb the familial atmosphere and the normality of life on a street to balance the hard day that she has just had. Hardwood is on the phone, chatting away cheekily in Spanish. Pam can hear the name Estrella repeated a few times in a teasing fashion.

The Sergeant is obviously organizing his evening.

Kids are running and playing in the dirt.

'Señora?'

Pam's horse is almost startled.

A scruffy but sweet looking boy has appeared from nowhere. He has an irresistible but sad smile and deep black eyes. His name is Ramiro. He wears a khaki vest which is too small for him, ripped blue jeans and a bandanna around his forehead like a mini version of John Rambo in First Blood.

'Señora Official?'

Pam does not stop her horse, she just leans forward.

'Tell me guapito.'

Ramiro giggles and dances around the walking horse, almost startling the tired animal. Pam is forced to stop, to avoid trampling the kid.

'What is the horse called?'

'Rainbow.'

'Rambo? Caray! ra ta ta ta ta...'

He mimics someone shooting with a big machine gun, the horse is startled, Pam gets Rainbow under control again.

'Rainbow like the arch of coloured light in the sky.' The boy changes expression, almost upset.

'I prefer Rambo, it is more macho.' Pam finds herself smiling, he is sweet.

'You can call him Rambo, I am sure it doesn't mind. What's your name?'

'Ramiro, but todos call me Rambo.' He strikes an aggressive pose. 'I could kill you. In town you're the law, out here it's me. Don't push it or I'll give you a war you won't believe.'

He says the lines from the film with a deep voice that almost resemble Stallone's. The boy must have seen the film many times. Pam is taken aback.

'Is that a real gun?' Pam nods affirmatively

'Have you ever used it?'

Pam is becoming uneasy, keeping an eye on the others riding ahead she just gives him a nod. More boys are now joining in.

'Si? Carlos!'

He calls out to another boy named Carlos, all dressed in black and wearing ridiculously big mirror sunglasses. He holds a large Polaroid camera.

'Take a photo hombre, that is a real gun that shoots real bullets.' Carlos positions himself and fires off a Polaroid of Pam with Ramiro next to the horse. The flash startles the horse, but Pam manages to calm it down. Pam spurs her horse.

'Yes it is, but now get out of the way because I am late.'

The boy keeps jumping in front of the horse; Pam is trying to negotiate around him. More boys are now copying what Ramiro is doing.

The horse is not happy having so many teasing kids around as well as feeling Pam's tension. The boy is now pulling faces right next to the animal's mouth.

'Caballito! Rambo hey! Why don't you kill me?'

'Get out of the way or you will get hurt.'

Pam is trying to move forward without trampling the kids. Suddenly there are too many of them all surrounding the horse, all teasing her. She makes eye contact with Hardwood and his men in the distance; they seem amused at her ordeal. They disappear into the maze of alleys. Pam moves the horse in circles, trying to steer the animal away from the children but it seems the children love it. They toss the Polaroid camera around taking pictures and enjoying seeing the horse becoming increasingly nervous.

Hearing all the commotion women and men are appearing at the windows above and at their front doors, some giggling and pointing at the mayhem the kids have created. Pam is edgy, almost as strongly as her horse is.

'Out of the fucking way!'

It's now chaos. Kids chanting and rattling off names at the horse; making gestures as if firing guns. Pam's horse is almost panicking; Pam is really struggling to keep it calm. She grabs her Motorola from her belt and tries to call for help on the radio, but both her hands are busy keeping the horse under control.

Some of the kids are now waving makeshift flags at the animal, long strips of fabric on sticks that they wave around at the horse, some make a hissing noise.

It is all too much even for a well-trained animal and suddenly the horse rears, neighing in an uncontrollable manner, fed up of all the taunting.

Pam nearly falls off; caught completely off guard, her radio flies to the ground and breaks into two. She struggles with knees and reins and eventually the horse calms down, panting and clearly stressed.

There is a surreal silence, only the heavy breathing of Pam's horse. All the kids are staring at one area of the street right next to the horse.

Ramiro, the boy that started all this, is lying motionless on the ground, face up, a pool of blood coming from his back wetting the cobbles.

Pam is in shock, the kids scatter away, disappearing into the alley ways. Pam is about to dismount when a woman screams her lungs out. 'She killed him! Madre Santissima! Ramiroooooooooo...'

The woman lunges towards the boy and lifts him with her arms. More people surface from the adjacent alleys, they seem to be coming out of nowhere; quickly they form a small crowd.

Pam shouts. 'Call an ambulance!'

The crowd is surrounding her. Baseball bats appear in the hands of few young men. A knife, a machete flashes amongst the bodies moving forward. It doesn't look good. Pam tries to pacify the crowd. 'Stay back! It was an accident.'

Her voice is increasingly trembling. Another knife appears in someone's hand, a chain is swinging from someone else's side. More people joining.

'My radio is broken, you must call an ambulance immediately.'

People are now completely surrounding her; the horse is feeling the tension and neighing, desperately wanting to go.

Pam is still trying to keep the peace. 'Someone call an ambulance!'

Everyone is staring at her, almost in a zombie like fashion slowly moving forward, wary of the horse. Suddenly there is a small opening in the crowd, Pam spurs her horse and makes for the opening, steering her horse down the steps of a nearby alley.

The horse jumps ahead negotiating the stairs, skidding crazily down the steps, nearly losing balance twice. Pam's shoulder catches some clothes hanging to dry from a balcony. Some men are chasing her waving machetes.

She whips her horse and heads flat out across the maze of alleys, the sound of an engine roaring behind her. As she turns, she spots two men on a motorcycle flying down the narrow street, the passenger is waving a machete. Further away there are more people on scooters with similar intentions.

Pam pulls the reins hard on Rainbow who nearly comes to a stop, and then she manages to get him to climb some very narrow and deep steps behind a fountain. The horse works hard its way up.

The motorcycle comes to a screeching halt. The rider swears and then spins around and goes back from where he came.

Pam is now bolting down an alley so narrow that the horse can barely get through. Suddenly at the opposite end she can see that a group of people are waving all sorts of blunt weapons block the alley.

She pulls the horse to a stop, it's too narrow to turn the horse around and she hears the sound of more people coming and blocking the way she came from.

She scans the alley and sees a double door on her right; she spurs Rainbow and makes him crash through the door.

As she crashes through the doors she ends up in a large space crammed with all sorts of goods, mostly TV sets, it is clearly someone's storage facility. Her sweat-lathered horse is circling trying to avoid the piles of stashed goods.

A light is switched on, and on the other side a door swings open. A man in his underpants is holding a gun. He is shocked to see that what he thought was thieves is in fact a CBP Officer complete with horse. Pam spurs poor Rainbow towards the man standing at the door.

'Get out of the fucking way !'

She's coming fast and furious towards him; he dives behind some boxes as Pam flies through on Rainbow, full of fear.

They fly past the terrified man emerging from the main shop doors into a little square. More alleys veer off in different directions. There is a small, derelict, dried up fountain in the middle. The sound of angry men approaching from different directions can be heard, growing closer.

'Fuck... Which one? Which one?' Multiple choice in a dangerous situation is not necessarily a good thing.

She makes a move for the alley right across, with great determination. As she has nearly passed the fountain, a battered Toyota pick up truck full of men careers into the square from exactly that way. She manages narrowly to steer a foam-flecked Rainbow into the one next to it.

She is now galloping at full speed; it seems that she has managed to shake her pursuers off. She pulls Rainbow to a walk, trying to get her bearings. The horse is exhausted, steaming.

'Good boy... good boy.'

She sees a car's headlights approaching from the opposite direction and decides to turn right. The horse seems to agree happily. Suddenly a screeching noise is coming from the main road.

The car is doing a U-turn at speed. Some shouts come from other directions.

There is the sound of a scooter approaching.

'Shit.' She takes a narrower street, going uphill and turns several times to lose the car into alleys that seem to get narrower. There is a real labyrinth of impossibly narrow lanes, the chaotic maze of downtown Saint Helena, the inner belly of the town.

All of a sudden she finds herself in a little courtyard, a familiar environment. She has a moment of realization when she sees the little tavern where she met Estrella. She is about to turn Rainbow around to go back when she hears a noise coming from high up. She looks at the roofs to see a giant black fabric falling from the roof, small fishing weights on the sides, enveloping her and Rainbow in darkness.

In the obscurity men jump on Pam and her horse as the cloth wraps around. They bring them both to the ground, the horse neighs frantically, the men start hitting the mass under the fabric with wooden bats.

She is waving her hands trying desperately to fend off the shower of blows. Rainbow is next to her neighing, then suddenly everything spins, goes out of focus, she passes out.

13. THE DEVIL'S POSSE

Pam's head is hurting, hurting badly.

Black is still filling her vision; it's hard to tell if the giant black cloth is still on her or if she just cannot see. She shivers. Squinting seems painful but she can make out something, something bright; a feeble light.

The light is dancing crazily, almost like a glowing jellyfish. As she tries to focus; the light becomes a light bulb, swinging from the ceiling. Her semi-conscious face is weathered.

Pale.

One eye is swollen and black.

Suddenly a hand comes down fast and slaps her; hard. The force of the blow rocks her head to one side. As she swings and spins she catches a glimpse of her new surroundings.

There are bare walls, dirty.

No furniture except a large block of stone in the middle with cast iron rings bolted on it and a chair occupied by a large man called Dago, slumped in it scratching his groin. He leans over and slaps Pam again. She stirs, her eyelids flutter.

Dago speaks in Spanish like a caveman, more a grunt than words. 'I think she is awake.' Another man's voice comes from behind her.

'Make sure.'

The man steps forward to face her; he is Rodolfo, standing next to the light bulb. He rhythmically taps it and makes it swing. His face is an impenetrable mask. He never smiles. He has no emotions.

Dago gets up and stands over Pam. He fumbles with his zip. Pam's expression is the one of a rabbit mesmerized by headlights. She blinks and is showered by a sudden burst of stinking yellow piss, Dago's piss.

Pam groans and tries to move out of the way, but Dago kicks her hard in the ribs. As she screams he centres her mouth with a burst of urine. She gurgles and spits it out. She feels another kick to her back, hard, painful. She recoils.

'Swallow it puta!' Pam coughs.

Rodolfo leans over her.

'I am comfortable here. Are you comfortable?'

She shakes her head. No. 'This is easy work for me. I know what I am doing and I am very good at it. I earn good money.' He walks around her.

'How much do you earn to sit on a horse and kill boys all day?'

She is terrified, can barely speak. 'I did not kill the niño.'

'Don't speak Spanish to me, it's not your language. I speak English. I don't collect food stamps and I am not lazy. I work. You see?' He flexes his biceps. Impressive. 'But you gringos always make jokes about Mexicans which ain't funny. I like jokes but they must have truth in them. The whole food stamps, job stealing and lazy Mexican crap isn't true and is contradicted by the next joke.' He clearly fancies the sound of his own voice. 'How can a Mexican be lazy on welfare when Mexicans are stealing all your jobs? You can't have it both ways. If there was a Latino out there not working and lazing all day it's probably an El Salvadorian, the lazy scum of Latin America, if you don't believe it, ask an old El Salvadorian.'

Rodolfo gestures to Dago who goes over to her and drags her to her feet. She is a trembling wreck. Rodolfo moves right next to her, inches away. He pulls out a knife and shoves it under her throat.

'Oh look, another stereotype, a Mexican with a knife, how funny. Do you know a funny joke about Mexicans, officer?' She stares ahead, terrified. 'No? What a shame.' He looks pensive, his perverse logic at work. 'I tell you what; if you can make me laugh I won't kill you. How's that?'

Dago cackles. She swallows hard, steadies herself. She takes a deep breath, summoning all her strength, what is left of it. Each word comes out like drops of blood.

'Why...'

Rodolfo narrows his eyes. Pam's voice is broken. This is not easy. 'Why... do Mexicans re-fry their beans?'

Dago moves closer ready for the punch line. 'Have you seen a Mexican do anything right the first time?'

A pause while the words still echo in the room; then Rodolfo starts laughing, really loud, almost loses it. Dago joins in, half-hearted, not quite sure.

'Now, that's funny. You are funny.' Rodolfo accompanies his words shooting his palm onto Pam's face lifting her off of the ground and dropping her flat on her back. Dago is laughing really hard now. That is what he considers funny. 'It's funny because it's true. I give you that.' Rodolfo's words echoed sinisterly.

She is lying on the floor, blood pouring from her mouth. Dago goes to her and picks her up like a rag doll. Her legs start to give way. He catches her and throws her back against the wall. He slaps her lightly in the face to revive her; she looks at him, then at Rodolfo as he comes closer.

'The truth is that Mexicans need to do things twice to get it right.' He cold-cocks her with his fist on her nose, breaking it. She collapses onto the floor, her face a bloody mess. Rodolfo kneels next to her, carefully observing her face; he even grabs her cheeks in his hands to examine her nose.

'Here, perfect second time round.'

Dago laughs loudly. His boss is very funny. 'I'll keep my promise. I won't kill you.'

Dago seems disappointed. 'But that doesn't mean you will live.'

Rodolfo points at a door. 'Behind that door there are more than one hundred men. They work hard all day in a sulphur mine nearby. They come back home and their women don't want to be fucked by them because they stink of devil's own. Have you ever smelled sulphur?'

Pam is gurgling blood through her lips then she shakes her head; no.

'It's vile. Some of these men haven't seen a woman for months. Because they know that even prostitutes won't let them near them, they stop washing themselves. The sulphur powder gets everywhere, encrusting their hair, their dicks. It hurts like hell. So what they came up with to relieve their urges is this room.'

He points at the stone in the middle.

'They bring a goat to the stone and tie the animal to the rings so it cannot move. Then they queue and they fuck the poor beast for hours. Once the last one is finished the animal is almost dead. Sometimes it is dead. Goats are very hardy animals.'

Dago grabs Pam by her hair and drags her to the stone. She tries to fight him off, but the huge Mexican is no match for her. He ties her to the stone, legs spread and her back to the stone.

'Because they feel sorry for the goat they normally make sure it is facing away. I want to make sure that you feel every single one's breath on you, and see their faces. You can beg but they won't listen, they know that you are the boy's killer.'

He moves towards her and pull her blouse off, ripping it apart. He then gestures to Dago who opens the door. A large group of men slowly enter the room. They are caked with red sulphur encrusted powder.

They are all touching their genitals to be ready, standing in a line.

Their grunts resemble pigs about to be fed. They move closer to a now screaming Pam. Rodolfo and Dago leave.

The first in the queue is an overweight, hairy guy. Behind him is a young and fit guy, almost sweet looking. The big hairy guy grabs Pam trousers and pulls them down. He is about to get to business when an old guy jumps out from behind the queue and shouts in gargled Spanish.

'What the fuck is going on?' He moves swiftly towards Pam pushing the big hairy guy out of the way. He unties Pam quickly and grabs her shoulder, the one with the tattoo.

'Are you all blind? What the fuck! Stay back dirty fuckers.'

Pam doesn't understand. She covers her breasts. The old guy helps her down. Everyone else moves back respectfully. Pam is begging with her last remaining energy, she really struggles.

'Por favor, let me go.'

The young fit guy who was second in line comes closer.

'You can go, we know who you are.'

Pam is now struggling physically and mentally.

'You saved a girl from being raped this morning. Everyone knows the officer with the tattoo did that. Nobody will touch you. Go now.'

The young guy hands her the blouse. She can barely walk but somehow makes it to the exit. She stumbles on the deserted street, pitch black. A horse is neighing nearby; and she hears the sound of hooves.

Rainbow is they're waiting for her. One of the miners is holding it. She struggles onto it, no fancy climbing, just a painful mount.

'Good boy... I am so glad to see you.' The horse moves, a slow walk. She sways on the saddle, everything hurts, every single bone. 'Easy, boy.' The horse slows down further.

There are no stars in the sky, no stars at all.

The night has a slight chill, refreshing for a bruised Pam, slipping in and out of consciousness. The street lamps and occasional sounds startle her. She clearly has no idea where she is going; she lets the horse decide the route. Eventually the horse stops outside Estrella's Tavern. Five men are talking to themselves outside the door. They look like the devil's posse.

'Madre de Dios!'

Pam is terrified, this cannot be true.

'No...no... Oh God....'

She tries to turn the horse around but one of the men is too quick and grabs the reins, while another tries to get to her. Another man shouts. 'No problemo!'

Rainbow rears startled by the men, neighing loudly.

'Don't sweat it!'

Pam loses her grip and falls on her back. The men are trying to catch her, laughing. She is out cold; this was too much, too much. Black, endless black fills her brain again. Slowly the darkness is glowing hot. The colour red fills her vision. The redness of what seems like blood.

Everything is red in colour. It's all vague; a blurred vision. There are these strange sounds coming from everywhere, words really, but they make no sense.

'...don't move..'

'...inexperienced...'

'...first day...'

'...training...'

The first thing she sees clearly is something deep red. It is definitely red. It takes a moment before she realizes it's a curtain hanging from a ceiling.

Now there's another one; Moroccan style.

It's Estrella's pad.

The smell of the beautiful Mexican is close, she smells like mint and honey. Estrella is standing beside Pam.

She wears a red robe and has a glowing complexion as if she just made love. She has pills in her hands and a glass of water.

Pam is motionless, swollen. She has a few scratches and a black eye. Her nose is busted; eyes are barely open and she tries to stand up.

She reaches for her holster but realizes her gun is missing. Hardwood's voice comes from a corner.

'You fucked up good.'

The Sergeant moves forward, towering over Pam.

He is holding Pam's Beretta by the barrel. 'I got your back, but this is seriously fucked up. If it wasn't for Estrella here they would have butchered and minced you and Rainbow up in one big pot.'

Estrella takes pity, this is not the way. 'Leave her alone. Here, take these.' Estrella pushes the pills into Pam's mouth with a sensual gesture, then hands her the glass. Pam gulps down the pills and water. She slowly gets up, sways, woozy. 'Lie down, rest.' Pam is trying to recollect what happened.

She staggers.

'My horse, where's my horse?'

Hardwood is still in cut-throat mood.

'Yeah, never mind the poor boy you pulped over, worry about the horse. Maybe the poor animal is hurt after mauling a ten year old boy with its hooves. You got your priorities right dontcha officer? You finally graduated.'

He cackles.

Pam's face is incredulous, then tears start running down her cheeks; she remembers. 'Is he...'

'The boy's body was gone when we turned up looking for you. They even washed the blood. Word on the street says you lost control.'

Hardwood seizes Pam; tears are running copiously, he sees her agony. His tone becomes softer, almost sympathetic. 'Those chicos die by the dozen here, they sniff glue and all sorts of shit.'

'Not him, not Ramiro. I want to report it.'

Hardwood hardens his jaw. 'I can hear your heart breaking but it's too late now to take care of the pieces. You should have done the right thing there and then. You freaked out and left a mess. You are lucky to be alive. Now be cool and play along.'

'I don't want to play along.'

Hardwood is a brick wall. 'Yes you do. We always look after our own.'

'I don't feel like one of your own.'

'The boys are feeling for you, you earned their respect.'

She gathers all her strength. 'Fuck you and your sidekicks, you don't have any idea what feelings are and you don't respect anything.'

She grabs the Beretta from Hardwood and holsters it. 'I will do the right thing and report to the captain. He'll understand.'

Hardwood is laughing. 'Report what? Wet pebbles? The only thing the captain will understand is four decorated experienced officers telling him that a greenhorn dyke is tripping under the sun.'

'We'll see about that.' She goes towards the stairs; stops. 'Maybe the Feds will love to have a one to one with the captain about Saint Helena or the content of white parcels.' She whips out her cell phone, pushes a few keys, turns it towards Hardwood. A short sequence starts playing. Alan's voice is coming out of the cell phone. 'That's a big one.'

Pam shows him a video on the small screen of Hardwood weighing a white package in his hand in Alan's sitting room. The recorded Sergeant's words come through loud and clear. 'You know it's a mountain I can't help climbing.'

She stops the playback, grinning.

Hardwood looks at Estrella. He bursts out laughing. Estrella shakes her head and disappears behind a thick oriental curtain. She comes back seconds later with the same parcel Pam has just shown Hardwood on the recording. She goes to Pam as Hardwood commands her to.

Pam is puzzled. 'What's this all about?'

'Open it and you will find out.'

'Drugs?'

'Open it.' Hardwood pulls out a Leatherman multi-tool from his belt, switches the blade open and hands it to Pam.

'Go ahead.'

Cautiously Pam opens the parcel. Inside is a bundle of photographs showing children, all ages, all Mexican. There are Mexican Police stamps all over always surrounding a big one saying DESAPARECIDO followed by a date.

'Oh God.'

Hardwood gets the pictures back. He starts flicking through them. 'God cannot help tracking down these children, because they don't have blonde hair, freckles and wealthy parents. In Saint Helena I found more than twenty in a ranch tied up in chicken sheds, some dead, some I wished were.'

These are clearly painful recollections even for a hard type like the Sergeant. 'There was one guy guarding them. I lost my temper; he lost his guts all over the ranch.' He clinches his fist. Hard.

'Problem is I made sure his body parts where detaching his body slowly, real slow, so that I could find out who was behind that hell. As it goes that live autopsy didn't go down too well with chair warming high ranks.'

'It was Alan who tipped me off about the ranch and it's thanks to Alan's devil work that I am still wearing a badge. But that devil knows way too much for him not to be involved somehow. I will find out eventually but at the moment I need him. The world is not just black and white officer is it?'

Pam is lost for words. 'We gotta stop this.'

'We? Are we "we" again now?' He blows Estrella a kiss and moves down the stairs. 'There is no "we".'

His words are still echoing as he disappears down the steps. Pam turns towards Estrella only in time to see one of her feet disappearing behind the heavy curtains. A strange noise comes from there, almost the sound of muffled crying. Pam negotiates the steps down to the exit as if crossing a creek; every step seems to have a mind of its own.

Her legs are giving way as if she has been running a marathon. King is holding her horse that looks as tired as Pam. She gets on the saddle using a stool to help her. Hardwood is staring, on another occasion an acerbic remark would have followed, this time with a tired look he watches Pam climb onto Rainbow.

Horses and men all move at once like a synchronised parade. Pam finds herself next to Hardwood; their horses must feel that is the way it should be by now. The others are ahead talking amongst each other.

Suddenly a boy runs out of a house and goes straight to the Sergeant. Hardwood leans over and the boy frantically says something in his ear. The boy tears off back where he came from.

Hardwood turns to Pam.

'There is something that you should see.' He whistles to his men. They turn their horses and join. Hardwood dismounts and heads towards a door. Pam looks puzzled and unsure. This day seems like it's never going to end. He disappears inside. Pam dismounts and follows the Sergeant in the modest house.

As her eyes adjust she can see a bunch of old women in a corner, praying quietly. They ignore Pam completely. Candles are burning everywhere. The noise of a baby crying grows from deeper inside.

Pam moves into the back room, uneasy.

In the bedroom a few more women are praying amongst more candles. A baby is sucking milk from a woman's breast. He makes the only sound in the room. The Sergeant has his back to Pam; leaning over a bed in the middle of the room. Pam moves closer.

As she reaches the Sergeant she sees young Ramiro's dead body lying on the bed, surrounded by flowers and candles.

The Sergeant is examining the body, there is a bullet wound on the boy's back. He must have died instantly. Hardwood speaks with no emotions.

Dead bodies, including those of the very young, must be a familiar sight. 'This is more fucked up than it was fucked up.'

Pam is gasping for air. 'I swear I did not fire.'

'I know.' He grabs a little brass plate on a side table. A bullet lies on it. 'The local vet removed it trying to save him.' He examines the bullet closer.

'This is a sniper's work. That's some cold shit.'

14. MARIMACHA

The barbed wire and the ugly concrete blocks never seemed so like home to everyone. The horses are drinking and grazing on some hay under a shed.

The checkpoint is very quiet; nobody seems willing to cross the border tonight. Border Officers are busy or pretending to be busy back and forth from the main building. Cooley has found a young female officer to impress with his tell of the day.

A paramedic is examining Pam. Hardwood is talking with a high-ranking officer. He is getting a bollocking. At the earliest opportunity he crosses over to Pam, as the Paramedic is finishing patching her up.

'You just earned a week off. Not bad for your first day.'

'I will be here tomorrow.'

She winches as the medic carries on.

'No you won't.'

Hardwood's tone becomes paternal, surprisingly warm. 'I need you at your peak after that; we have a war to finish. Make sure you're not late.'

Pam smiles weakly. 'I can't be late until I show up.'

Hardwood smiles and walks away.

The sky is black like tarmac, there are no stars tonight; nothing shines. Slowly even the last remaining officers relax at the checkpoint; no cars on the horizon, not even coyotes are howling.

Hours slip by, another day comes and turns dark again, time seems tired of its own tempo.

The new night seems tired too; the desert has worn out everything and everyone. As the sun is rising over the cold hills, predawn has disappeared a while ago, if ever there was one this time.

A Chevrolet Pick Up is parked outside a familiar silver trailer, covered in desert morning dew; Pam's trailer.

A coyote was sleeping underneath. Suddenly the animal decides it's time to start the day somehow. Pam is listening to the news.

'...at the scene. The FBI is sweeping the grounds looking for clues of what seems to be a..' Pam is lying in bed. Her face is healing, she looks much better.

A few days have passed.

She is totally absorbed watching the news report.

A tear is slowly staining her left eye; grows bigger; runs down her cheek.

On the TV screen a reporter is doing her piece to camera. In the background there is a flurry of ambulances and police cruisers. There are men in uniform and the odd detective in a suit flashing a badge.

There is mayhem on the pristine looking lawn, next to a swimming pool. A body is floating in the water and men in white CSI overalls are fishing it out.

The reporter is speaking to camera, another day at work; just names on a prompter.

'The FBI is not releasing any statements at the moment but a deputy told us that the body count is definitely five. This includes, as previously reported, highly decorated CBP officer, Sergeant Mike Hardwood and three of his men and retired government official Alan Macy. The hunt is on for Rodolfo Gonzalez' A mug shot of Rodolfo appears on the screen. 'A drug baron involved in kidnapping two young boys in Austin last week. The dynamics of the shoot-out are not clear yet but the FBI has confirmed that this afternoon there will be a statement released at the Sheriff's office. This is Kathy Miller reporting live from Macy's Ranch near...'

Pam's cell phone rings. The Mexican ballad ring tone. She answers.

'Yes sir.' 'I will, thank you sir. I am on my way. There was no need for that.' She listens more. 'That's appreciated.'

She hangs up. She puts on her utility belt and is about to leave when the door suddenly bursts open and a bubbly overexcited Stephanie storms the room.

'Hi sis, he wants to marry me! He said he wants to marry me! Oh my God!' She hugs Pam in a avalanche of excitement. She stops; looking carefully at Pam, noticing her tears.

'Sorry did I just squeeze some broken ribs? Sorry! Oh God! Are you in pain?' She wipes a tear from Pam's cheek with her little finger. 'I love you.' She goes to the coffee jug and pours some in a cup.

'There is a Police car outside; I think he is waiting for you. The officer is so cute.' Stephanie giggles cheekily, Pam is not listening. She puts her boots on.

'Don't wait for me later, I might have a long day.' Pam's words come out tired and struggling.

Stephanie is hyper. 'Ah yes I heard it on the radio, it's all over the news! Did you know that-'

She turns towards her sister but Pam has left the trailer.

The day is just starting and the sun is already glowing hot. The CBP cruiser is just outside. A clean cut young officer is waiting for Pam. Stephanie is right; he is cute, very cute and very green. He is very nervous too, in an overly keen manner.

'Morning ma'am'. I am here to...' He stops; Pam is already in the car.

'Sorry, I didn't... Good morning, are you comfortable? It must hurt... still. I guess. I brought a coffee and donuts from HQ, I thought you might, I didn't-'

'Is this your first day?' The rookie cop jumps in the seat and starts the car.

'Yes ma'am. But I learn fast.' He gives her a good look, sees the scars. Pam looks much older now. 'I mean no disrespect ma'am, you are... I mean you have worked there a few years right?'

'Twenty four...'

The rookie whistles interrupting her. Pam finishes her sentence darting a disapproving look. 'I have been with the unit twenty four hours.'

The rookie officer is startled, but then drives off thinking that she is winding him up or testing him. It cannot be, Pam definitely looks like a veteran. As he stomps on the gas pedal Stephanie runs out of the trailer and is nearly run over by the cruiser speeding off.

The car screeches to a halt in a cloud of dust.

'Shit.'

The rookie managed to steer and avoid her. Stephanie goes to Pam's side and with a smooth move drops unnoticed Pam's Beretta into her lap.

'The part you always want to leave behind. Have a good day sis!' Stephanie's cell phone rings, she answers in no time. 'Hi Jake... Miss me? What do you mean no wedding cake?'

She disappears through the door giggling.

Pam smiles watching her sister go back into the trailer. She holsters her gun and gestures the rookie cop to drive.

The cruiser leaps forward munching tarmac along the desert interstate; a long strip of ugly black cutting through dust. The car is speeding in the beautiful but bare landscape. The sun is now bathing everything in gold. Inside the car Pam is deep in thought, or so it seems.

The light is startling the rookie driver who is struggling to put his Rayban on. Pam grabs the wheel so he can use two hands. The young cop is quick getting back to the driving business.

'Thank you. Not used to this desert light yet.'

There is a long silence.

Is this going to be a one-way conversation? The rookie officer tries something different.

'That's your sister right? She is very nice. She's getting married soon I heard; hopefully to someone with a proper job.'

Pam sighs. 'She is marrying a jura.' The rookie cop is puzzled.

'That's Mexican for cop. Do you speak Spanish officer?'

'Yo speak un poquito...'

Pam interrupts him briskly. 'Better brush up your shit if you want to know what they are talking about when you frisk them.' She is annoyed. The young cop is quite embarrassed but quickly settles. The sedan cruises along. They are both silent. The rookie spots something in the distance, on Pam's side; he leans forward to focus better on what it is.

'On your ten. That is one big ugly coyote!'

Pam leans to have a better look. On a crest of a nearby hill a large white dog is observing as they drive past. A Doberman, a white Doberman. Four coyotes appear on its sides, submissive, the white Doberman is clearly in charge. The Doberman is clearly Blanko. Pam is still taken aback by what she's seen.

The rookie is very excited.

'It's a fuckin dog! He won't survive in such a hostile environment.'

Pam sighs deeply. 'They can if they adapt and change to survive. They become what surrounds them. If you live among coyotes you cannot act like a dog.' The rookie is impressed by Pam's wisdom. The cruiser's tyres churn up more road.

'Will you teach me some Mexican slang?' The young cop is feeling brave.

'Maybe, over dinner?' Pam is smiling lightly.

Madre this hombre is green.

'Sure.'

A smile appears on her broken lips. 'Marimacha.'

The rookie officer tries his best. 'Maa-ri-maa-cha... cool. What does it mean?'

A pause. Pam knows she is going to enjoy this. 'Tomboy. It means tomboy.' The cruiser is speeding off the black tarmac; in the distance the border with Mexico is just visible.

'But it can also mean dyke.'

Pam says it with a tired smile, her words swirl inside the car like the dust that covers everything, including the long line of vehicles of all sorts queuing up at the checkpoint.

About the Author

Francesco Pagot was born near Venice, Italy not California, and was educated in the classics. His celluloid addiction brings him to Milan, where he works all sorts to support his habit. In 1989 he moved to London, eventually establishing himself as a cinematographer.

After winning a Creative Review writing competition he intensified his efforts, writing screenplays that have won awards, produced and sold. Greenhorn is his first novel. He lives in London.